A Cowboy's Calm Strength

Sweet View Ranch Western Christian Cowboy Romance Book Six
Jessie Gussman

Published By: Jessie Gussman

This is a work of fiction. Similarities to real people, places, or events are entirely coincidental. Copyright © 2024 by Jessie Gussman.

Written by Jessie Gussman.

All rights reserved.

No portion of this book may be reproduced in any form without written permission from the publisher or author, except as permitted by U.S. copyright law.

Contents

Acknowledgments — V

1. Chapter 1 — 1
2. Chapter 2 — 9
3. Chapter 3 — 20
4. Chapter 4 — 29
5. Chapter 5 — 38
6. Chapter 6 — 54
7. Chapter 7 — 63
8. Chapter 8 — 74
9. Chapter 9 — 85
10. Chapter 10 — 92
11. Chapter 11 — 102
12. Chapter 12 — 111
13. Chapter 13 — 121
14. Chapter 14 — 130
15. Chapter 15 — 138
16. Chapter 16 — 145
17. Chapter 17 — 152

18.	Chapter 18	162
19.	Chapter 19	175
20.	Chapter 20	182
21.	Chapter 21	194
22.	Chapter 22	206
23.	Chapter 23	213
24.	Chapter 24	225
25.	Chapter 25	229
26.	Chapter 26	235
27.	Chapter 27	241
28.	Chapter 28	244
29.	Chapter 29	251
30.	Chapter 30	254
A Gift from Jessie		256
Escape to more faith-filled romance series by Jessie Gussman!		257

Acknowledgments

Cover art by Julia Gussman
Editing by Heather Hayden
Narration by Jay Dyess
Author Services by CE Author Assistant

Listen to a FREE professionally performed and produced audiobook version of this title on Youtube. Search for "Say With Jay" to browse all available FREE Dyess/Gussman audiobooks.

Chapter 1

Phoebe tapped her finger on the metal bar. She had been curious about a lot of things in her life, but one of the things she had never wondered about was what life looked like from behind the vertical, cold steel bars of prison.

She had found out anyway.

"Rich, how much longer?"

"You know you're like a two-year-old on a car trip, right?" Rich said from where he sat behind the big corner desk, his feet propped up on the one spot that wasn't covered with papers, old take-out wrappers, and bottles of pain pills. He held a steaming cup of coffee in one hand with his other hand hooked on his belt loop, his fingers resting lightly over the radio clip there.

"I'm sorry. If you hadn't taken my watch, I wouldn't need to ask." Phoebe felt like a petulant child. She understood that the lock-in was supposed to simulate real life. When she agreed to do it for the Sweet Water High fundraiser, she figured it wasn't going to be a walk in the park, and neither did she expect that.

Originally it was supposed to be on a Friday night, but the jail had been too crowded, so it had been moved to a weekday. She appreciated that. But it was almost time for her to be let out, and she didn't want to stay one second longer than what she had to.

She'd signed up for twelve hours, found ten people to pledge ten dollars an hour, and had raised twelve hundred dollars for the high school. But twelve hours was it.

Rich was not the kind of guy who was going to be early or even super concerned about letting her out on time. It was up to her.

"We don't allow regular prisoners to keep their watches, so why would we let you keep yours? This is supposed to be the real deal."

"I know. I won't ask again, if you'll just let me know how much longer." She made that promise, hoping she could keep it. Surely it had been at least an hour since she'd asked the last time, and at that point, she'd had one hour and twenty-seven minutes left.

"You promise?" Rich said with a brow raised.

"I do."

"And if you break your promise, what do I get?"

She almost huffed out a breath. She was thirty-six years old and not exactly the kind of person who inspired romantic interest in men. She'd figured that out a long time ago, back in her twenties when she was raising her siblings and no one was interested in her.

She'd given up the idea that she would ever get married. And maybe, after what her twin had gone through with her marriage, it had been a good decision. Although she would have liked to have had a husband and children. She wanted that. But it seemed like God had her serving her own family, her brothers and sisters, and stepping in after her parents had died. She mostly accepted that and didn't long for a family of her own.

Much, anyway.

"What do you want?" she asked with resignation.

"You ask me again, and you're gonna watch my kids next Friday night while I go on a date."

"Done," she said easily. Yeah, she didn't think he was actually going to want her to do anything with him. Just watch his kids.

So, one night in the lockup hadn't changed anything in that regard.

She waited while he pulled his phone out of his front shirt pocket and tilted it so it kicked on, trying not to be impatient.

He said the time, and she calculated in her head that she had twenty-three minutes left.

Monday night had been a good choice, since there hadn't been any other...prisoners? Patrons? What was it called when a person was put in jail?

Anyway, she had been alone all night, which had been just fine with her, although she wouldn't have minded keeping her phone at the very least. She could read a book or something. As it was, she'd occupied herself by staring at the cell wall while trying not to think about how dirty the mattress was behind her. Or how many other people had slept on it.

It wasn't that the jail was filthy, because it wasn't. Not really. Not compared to their barn on the ranch. But she figured out that she was a little claustrophobic and more of a germaphobe than she wanted to admit. At least when it came to prison cells. Who knew?

Sighing, she turned away from the bars, walked back over, and sat down on the mat where she'd spent most of the last twelve hours. Drawing her feet up, she leaned back against the wall. She hadn't slept very well, and she was tired, but she had a full morning's worth of work to do when she got released.

Her family had been working hard to make their dude ranch a success, and they'd decided to host a rodeo this year. It would draw people in, let people know about the ranch, and hopefully get them some bookings for next spring and summer. If not this fall. Cold came to North Dakota early, but fall was still a beautiful time of year here.

Winter was pretty too, and they were thinking about getting some draft horses and doing sleigh rides at least through the holiday season.

But Phoebe had been put in charge of the rodeo.

Her, along with a new guy that they had hired just for that…to coordinate the rodeo and help them run it. They were planning on keeping him on as a full-time employee afterward, if things went well.

Tillman Snyder was the man's name, and he was supposed to show up at the ranch first thing this morning.

Phoebe didn't know much else about him other than he had been her brother's college roommate and her brother, Ezra, had asked her to work with him to get things organized. She was known as being particular and meticulous in recordkeeping, plus she would organize the food and games and prizes as well as the decorations and the arrangements on the ranch, while he took care of all of the things that she didn't really know much about—the events themselves, getting the temporary corrals and everything else set up, and she didn't even know what all else.

But hopefully, Tillman and she would be able to combine their strengths and make the rodeo a smashing success. To say that the future of their ranch depended on it wasn't an overexaggeration.

She tapped her hand on her leg, figuring that twenty-three minutes had gone by long ago, but she'd promised she wasn't going to ask again.

Stealing a glance underneath her lashes at Rich, she wondered if he was deliberately not telling her her time was up so that she would ask again, so he'd have a free babysitter Friday night. She wouldn't put it past him.

Finally, she got up, and while she wasn't much of a pacer, she walked over to the end of the jail cell and back. She hadn't realized that she was claustrophobic. Last night had told her that much. That was probably the reason she wanted out more than anything. She had been trying to keep her mind occupied, thinking about other things, paramount among those the rodeo, but now that she knew her time was surely up, the walls felt like they were closing in, and it drove her crazy that she couldn't escape.

Not to mention, she had to use the bathroom, and she was absolutely not using the urinal that the cell provided.

She supposed she could probably complain. Surely there were discrimination laws that stated that a female prisoner needed to have facilities that suited her physiology. And privacy as well.

But considering that it was only twelve hours and that her time was up, she would be happy if Rich would simply let her out.

She went over and stood as close to him as she could get, trying to remind him that she was there, and it was time for her to leave.

He pretended not to notice.

She knew he was pretending, because she saw his eyes glance up and his lips quirk a little, and then he looked back down at the iPad that was balanced above his knees after taking a sip of his coffee.

Smelling the coffee made her stomach rumble and her mouth water. She usually started the day with at least two cups, but no one had offered her coffee. Or food of any kind.

Not that she had expected anything. After all, the jail was allowing them to do this as a matter of public service and kindness; she didn't want to cost the county any extra money.

She drew a breath in through her nose and blew it out her mouth. She was not going to say anything. And then she thought, why not? Did it really matter if she went to wherever Rich lived and watched his kids for an evening? It wasn't like she was typically super busy on Friday night. But she wasn't going to if she didn't have to.

"Rich?"

His head drew up slowly, and there was a small smirk, arrogant and irritating, that turned up the corner of one of his lips. "Are you asking me what time it is? Because, you do remember our deal, correct?"

"Correct. I remember. And you're right. I'm not asking, but if you happen to check…"

He gave her a look, knowing that now that she'd mentioned it, he could hardly continue to keep her past her time. With a put-out sigh, he uncrossed his legs and dropped them to the floor, grabbing the large key that worked the lock. She had expected everything to be electronic. Although, she hadn't really thought about whether or not the jail in Rockerton, North Dakota, would have entered the twenty-first century. If she had thought about it, she would have expected there to be some kind of electronic locks. But there wasn't.

"Aren't you going to look at your phone?" she asked.

"Don't need to. The timer on the desk that they set when the kids locked you in here last night went off twenty minutes ago."

"I didn't hear it."

"That's because I shut it off before it could go off."

"You did it on purpose?"

"Yeah?" he said, not bothering to try to hide his smirk. "You have no idea how expensive babysitters are nowadays."

She wanted to say something about the word sucker being stamped on her forehead and she didn't know it, but she didn't. She also tried to push away the thought that when a man looked at her, he saw sucker and babysitter, not siren and kissable, or any other romantic words, which showed how pathetic she was. She didn't even know any romantic words that she could use to describe herself.

Instead, she waited while he opened her cell door, then kept her irritation in check when he asked for her phone number—in case he needed a babysitter, a paid one—and programmed it into his phone.

"I'll give you a call at some point to see if you can watch the kiddos for me."

She nodded, then as she was sticking her phone back in her pocket, she said, "I could be a serial killer, you know."

He laughed. "I watched you for the last twelve hours. I definitely trust my kids with you. You're harmless and more than a little boring." He grinned. "No offense. That's actually a compliment, since I'm thinking about hiring you to watch my children."

She nodded, not liking the way her life had turned out, exactly, but laughing to herself that he had pinned her so correctly. She was serious, responsible, and, yeah, boring.

But at least she had made twelve hundred dollars for the Sweet Water high school. Even if she did end up with a babysitting gig she really didn't want because of it.

She shook her head. She wasn't going to have time to babysit, not if they were going to get the rodeo planned now and set up in two short months. She could always say no when he called.

She had to admit, as she stepped out of the jailhouse and started down the steps, that it felt great to be outside. Hopefully the little bit of claustrophobia she felt while locked up was not something that was going to erupt into a full-blown issue.

Maybe she'd been cooped up for too long, or maybe she was hungrier than she thought, because as she stepped down the steps, lifting her eyes to the sky and taking a deep breath of the warm late spring air, she lost her balance and started tumbling down the steps.

Chapter 2

Tillman Snyder walked down the street in Rockerton, North Dakota. He was supposed to meet his new boss at noon, and he had a few errands he needed to run in what he understood to be the closest large town to Sweet Water, which was the location of the ranch where he had been hired to coordinate a rodeo. The job was right up his alley; rodeos ran in his blood. But he was used to owning his own ranch, not working for someone else.

His divorce had changed the financial situation in which he saw himself. His wife had insisted on splitting everything right down the middle, and he hadn't had the financial resources to buy the ranch outright nor save his prized herd of horses. The alimony agreement had wiped him out.

So he sold his horses and the ranch as well. It pained him to lose everything he'd worked all his life for, but what good was a ranch if he had no family to share it with?

He flexed his jaw and continued down the sidewalk, glancing across the street at a lawyer's office beside a dentist and financial services.

On his side of the street, the jail loomed up, the old building perched at the top of about six steps.

A woman had started down the steps, and he slowed his stride almost imperceptibly so that she would pass in front of him, and neither of them would have to stop.

Focusing on the items that he needed to get done before he started his new job, he almost missed the blur of motion as the woman, apparently still tipsy from her lockup the night before, lost her balance on the steps, her arms windmilling as she took two steps in quick succession, trying to catch her balance as she careened down the steps.

He moved without thinking about it, lunging forward, reaching his arms out, and grabbing the woman before she crashed to the sidewalk.

It looked like they let her out a little too soon. She could have used a few more hours to sober up.

Except she didn't smell like alcohol. She smelled like apples in spring and laughter around the campfire.

He blinked, shaking his head a little, as he carefully steadied her before dropping his hands and stepping back.

"I'm so sorry!" the woman said, her cheeks pink, her eyes horrified. He would assume from the expression on her face that she didn't typically get so drunk that she couldn't walk a straight line or keep her balance.

"No problem, ma'am," he said, tipping his hat. He intended to go around her, but she swayed, and while he was tempted to roll his eyes and fought to tamp down his irritation, he still couldn't let a woman fall down in front of him, no matter how inebriated she was.

Nor should it matter how good she smelled.

In fact, the better she smelled, the more he would be tempted to walk away from her. Nicole always smelled good.

But not like this woman. His ex did not have the fresh, wholesome scent of western sky and rain on flower petals.

Still, he didn't know why her scent moved him so much when her actions irritated him beyond words. Nicole enjoyed her alcohol as well.

Her shoulder bumped against his chest, and if possible, her cheeks burned even brighter than they had before.

"I'm so sorry. I'm not sure what's wrong with me, other than I guess I was sitting too long."

"Maybe you shouldn't drink so much, then you won't have such a hard time sleeping it off."

He didn't mean to sound surly, but he supposed he probably did. She acted like he wouldn't know she was drunk.

Of course, he didn't smell alcohol. When his dad had come home smashed, he'd always been able to smell it on him.

The woman froze, her eyes shooting to his as she placed a hand solidly on his chest and pushed off him.

"I don't drink," she said, but her voice sounded confused, like she was asking a question instead of making a statement.

His lips pressed together at the obvious lie.

"Of course you don't," he said, giving her another couple of seconds to make sure she had her feet under her that time before he tipped his hat again. "Have a nice day, ma'am."

He didn't want to have an argument, and he didn't want to get into a fight with a stranger on the street. Especially a drunk stranger. Especially a drunk *female* stranger.

He didn't want to have anything to do with females, drunk or otherwise.

Not after what Nicole had done to him.

Pain shot through him at the thought of his two children. They were seven and nine, and he'd had such plans for the things they would do together as they grew.

He wanted to swear and use Nicole's name in the middle of it, but he pressed his lips even tighter together as he strode away.

He wasn't going to blame the bad things that happened in his life on anyone but himself.

Of course, he'd done everything he could to stop Nicole from divorcing him, but he was the one who had chosen her to begin with. He should have known someone that beautiful wouldn't have been able to stay with just one man. He'd been so honored when she chose him, but his life would have gone a much different and better direction if she'd passed over him for someone else.

He finished doing the things he'd come to town for, opening a checking account and getting his driver's license changed from Montana to North Dakota, and then headed out to the Sweet View Ranch.

It was still raw, losing his own ranch, and felt a bit like a comedown in the world to be working on someone else's, rather than making decisions on his own spread.

Lord, I didn't realize that I needed so many lessons in humility. I'd really like to learn my lessons this time, so You don't feel like You need to put me through this again.

He stopped at the gate, looking at the arch that said Sweet View Ranch in burnt metal, dark against the bright blue sky as he hooked his truck in gear and drove under.

It was the same kind of gate that he had at his own ranch, high enough for a tractor to go under and both a welcome and an announcement for everyone who came.

Shoving the bitter feelings aside, he focused on the job he was here to do. His dream of owning his own ranch had been yanked away from him, for now. Who knew how the Lord would work, and even if he never owned his own spread again, at least he hadn't had to take a job behind a desk under fluorescent lights in an office with no windows somewhere in a concrete jungle.

He still got to work outside, under the wide North Dakota sky, feel the wind ruffle through his hair and the heat of the sun on his face. Smell the pureness of the country air and work with his hands doing what he loved.

Even if Nicole had ripped his life away from him, God had been good.

Sorry for complaining, Lord. Help me to be an asset to this ranch. Help me to be the kind of worker that I would have wanted to hire. Help me to give a full day's work, and more, for what I get paid. Thank you for the opportunity. Help me to be grateful, and…help me to forgive.

He definitely needed help with that last one. He couldn't even think about Nicole without bitterness rising up in his throat.

There was a sign that said "office" and pointed toward the big farmhouse that sat a small distance from the other outbuildings. A smaller house sat directly behind it. Perhaps someone's residence.

He shut his pickup off, the one thing from his farm that he'd been able to afford to purchase when Nicole had insisted they auction everything off, and got out, taking the steps two at a time and debating for half a second before he opened the door and walked in.

"Hello, the house," he said, realizing that he had walked into someone's living room.

The sign had said *office*.

"Come on in," a female voice called from down the hall, from what he assumed was the kitchen.

"Sorry, ma'am. I thought the office pointed here."

"It does. We live here, too."

"If I'd have known that, I would have knocked."

"It's no big deal. We're expecting you," she said, coming out of the kitchen with one hand out, the other hand holding a tea towel. "I am Alaska, and you must be Tillman."

"I am. Good to meet you, Alaska," he said, recognizing her as the woman he talked to a couple of times on the phone.

Ezra's wife.

Ezra and he had been good friends and roommates in college. He had to admit he was a little surprised by the way Alaska looked. Not that there was anything wrong with her, she just didn't look like the kind of woman that his straightlaced, serious, line-walking friend from school would have dated, let alone married.

Maybe it was the tattoo sleeves, or the piercings, or the fact that the ends of her hair were platinum blond while darker roots grew in. Regardless, she seemed friendly and welcoming, and he figured she must have a character that was above reproach, if Ezra had fallen for her.

"Ezra will be here shortly, he was helping the guys with a couple of calves who'd gotten tangled up in some wire."

"All right," he said.

"If you want to come on into the kitchen and sit down, you're welcome to. I have some cookies cooling on the counter, and you're welcome to help yourself."

"Thanks, but if it's okay with you, I'll walk back out and wait on the porch. It's a nice day out. I won't go nosing around, but I'll see what I can see from there."

He didn't want to be stuck in the kitchen with Alaska, didn't want to eat cookies and feel like he was part of the family. It might be healing and peaceful for someone else, but for him, it would just feel like acid on an open wound.

That was what he had wanted. That was what he thought he was getting when he got married to Nicole. He'd had a rude awakening, because that was definitely not what he had gotten.

Alaska's face did not fall, and her smile stayed in place. She wasn't offended that he preferred to go outside. Maybe she even understood. Alaska knew a little bit about his background, at least the fact that he lost his ranch in his divorce and was looking for a place to work, something steady so that he could go back to the judge and try to get the custody arrangement changed. Since he had lost his job when they sold the ranch, the judge had given him visitation but no actual time to have the children. It would be kind of hard to do that when he didn't even have a house.

He could have made it work, though. And he tried to tell the judge that, but Nicole had been very convincing, that not only was he a terrible husband, but he was an awful father as well. He had wanted to prove her right, at times, by leaping over the table and grabbing her by the throat.

Her smug looks, her gloating when she had won, like their children were something that they should have been fighting over to begin with. He hadn't been able to reason with her, and nothing he had said had made a difference. You'd have thought she was trying to show off for her new boyfriend, Elbert.

Because of her, he'd lost the ranch that he worked for his whole life. But more than that, he lost his children as well. Sure, he had visitation, but considering that he lived six hours away from them now, they could hardly come over for an evening after school, and even spending the weekend with them would be hard.

He wanted to go back to court and redo the visitation, since trying to talk to his ex was virtually useless.

His whole life, up in smoke. And through no fault or desire of his own. He had wanted to make things work, he had been willing to do whatever it took, but she hadn't been interested. She tossed him away like an old shoe, blew up his life without a second thought, and went to do whatever made herself happy.

He realized his hands gripped the railing so tightly his knuckles were white.

He deliberately loosened his hands and looked out over the wide expanse of the North Dakota landscape. Beyond the buildings of the ranch, grass blew in the wind as far as he could see until it met the long, low line of the sky in the distance.

There was something about that view that stirred his heart and soul and made him want to be better. In some small way. It also made him feel very small. Tiny, useless almost. And part of him wanted to acknowledge the majesty and glory of the Creator who made and controlled such a vast area. An area which was, in the grand scheme of things, quite small.

But if God controlled everything, why had He allowed his wife to walk away? Why was He allowing his children to grow up without him? Why had He allowed the ranch that had been the one dream in his life to be ripped away from him and sold?

Now, he was relegated to working for someone else, because the only thing he knew how to do was ranch and rodeo.

Swallowing hard, he turned away from the view, the desire to move forcing him to turn and start pacing across the porch.

He couldn't help it, his stride stopped abruptly when he saw his friend Ezra walking beside the woman who had run into him outside of the jail earlier that morning.

Figures.

That was the way his life was going lately. Of course she would be on the ranch for some reason. Hopefully she didn't work here.

Maybe she was a guest, one who was hopefully leaving soon.

Ezra said something, and she laughed, and Ezra, his taciturn and very serious friend, cracked a smile. Life had been hard for Ezra, with his parents dying and leaving twelve children with no mother or father and a huge ranch that needed to be taken care of, and all of the duties had fallen squarely on Ezra's shoulders, but it looked like he'd come full circle and maybe gotten some peace.

Maybe that had something to do with getting married. Tillman had heard that such a thing was possible. When a man got married, his work was halved, he had a partner to share his life with, share the burden with, someone to walk beside him, to ease her burden while she eased his, and somehow that made life easier for both of them.

That had not been his experience. Getting married had been the worst mistake he'd ever made in his entire life, and he could guarantee anyone that he would not be going down that trail again.

"Tillman! I thought you'd be inside with my wife eating cookies. She likes to load anyone who comes up with sugar if they step foot into her kitchen."

"She tried. You know me. I'd rather be outside."

He couldn't stand the stifling, happy family atmosphere of the house. Not with his own dreams of home and family still smoldering in ashes around his feet.

"That's part of what makes you good at what you do," Ezra said, having no problem understanding Tillman would prefer to be outside, never questioning it.

Ezra had known Tillman before he had been burned, multiple times, by his wife. And before Tillman had gotten bitter about everything. He didn't want to be bitter, didn't want to spend the rest of his life in bitterness, but he had never really sat down and thought about what it would take for him to not feel bitter anymore.

It wasn't like he could go back and redo the past. All he could do is all he could ever do, just keep moving forward. So he supposed, if he were to really think about it, there would be no solution.

Chapter 3

Ezra and the woman beside him reached the steps, and Tillman shifted his hat on his head.

It was then that the woman's strides stumbled. He wore a nondescript button-down shirt, along with jeans and boots. With the hat on his head, he probably looked like any other cowboy she had run into that day. In fact, his shirt wasn't that much different from the slightly lighter blue plaid shirt that Ezra wore.

Her pink sweatshirt acted like a beacon and made it easy for him to recognize her. That, and she didn't wear a hat. Her long hair still flowed down past her shoulders.

Plus, she was tall for a woman, coming up to Ezra's chin. Which would mean that she would fit just perfectly under his as he and Ezra were about the same height.

He shook the thought away. He was not tucking any woman under his chin, not ever again. Women were trouble. Heartbreak. All the bad things that he could think of. They weren't trustworthy, they were fickle, and he wanted to say that he hated them, but that would mean that he hated half the world's population. Although, at the moment, he supposed it was true.

"Tillman, I'd like to introduce you to my sister, Phoebe. I don't know if you remember that I had twin sisters right behind me in birth order. Phoebe is the older of the two, and this ranch couldn't run without her. She… She was right beside me when our parents died and shouldered as much of the burden as I did."

"I don't know whether I would go that far, and those days are over and past," Phoebe said with a smile that, while it reached her eyes, looked a little strained. "I actually already met Tillman today."

"You did?"

"I didn't realize who it was," Phoebe said easily as she stepped forward with her hand out.

Tillman took it in his, her fingers long and slender and cool to the touch. He shook it, a perfunctory shake that he knew he couldn't get out of without being rude, but dropped it immediately, and stepped back in the guise of leaning a hip against the banister.

"We met as she was coming out of the jail this morning," Tillman said, surprised that she could be so self-possessed and confident when she had obviously been locked up the night before. At least she didn't appear to be inebriated anymore.

"Oh. Interesting the folks you meet in jail, isn't it?" Ezra said with a grin that would never have flown back in the days when Tillman knew him. Ezra would have had the same reaction he had to anyone being thrown in jail. Not that he thought that a person who was in jail couldn't be a good person, but they'd obviously made mistakes that showed that if they didn't have a lot of character, they had a distinct lack of judgment at the very least.

Ezra and Phoebe, however, laughed at Ezra's comment like it was hilarious. Phoebe nodded. "Sure is. Although, I hopefully won't be there again for a very long time."

For some reason, this made Ezra laugh again, which Tillman had a difficult time explaining to himself. Had Ezra changed that much? Back when Tillman had known him, he had been an upright man, and while not perfect, he had clearly wanted to serve the Lord and point people to Jesus with his life. In everything he did, he had had character and integrity and had inspired the people around him to have the same.

But now, he was laughing with his sister about her spending the night in jail? Or maybe the week? Tillman didn't know when she had gone in. He just assumed she'd been locked up the night before at least.

"Phoebe will be the one that you'll be working with on the rodeo. She doesn't know anything more about it than I do. So, I'm not teaming her up with you because of her vast knowledge of how the rodeo works. That's all on you."

"That's what I thought," Tillman said.

"Rather, she's very organized and good with details. She catches on quickly, and she's familiar with every single thing around the ranch, just as familiar as I am, and not to belittle you, but I would say she's just as good as you are too. We've just never been around the rodeo."

"I understand. If she grew up on the ranch, that makes sense."

"Yes. And she's been running, first our ranch in Wyoming and now this one, with me for a decade and a half."

"He gives me more credit than I deserve," Phoebe said with an easy smile. "I spend a lot of time in the kitchen. Cooking and doing the cleanup and the grocery shopping for full-time ranch workers is not easy."

"And she helped homeschool our younger siblings once our parents passed away."

Phoebe nodded, and a little bit of the glow faded out of her face, but she didn't say anything more.

He had to cut her a little slack. Anyone who had lost their parents the way they had, with a family their size, maybe didn't deserve to have a lapse of judgment but could be forgiven for one.

Of course, he'd had a major lapse of judgment, and he would like to be forgiven for that too. Although the only one that really needed to forgive him was himself. He still took himself to task for being so ridiculously naïve when it came to Nicole.

Never again.

"Phoebe will be working hand in hand with you, by your side. The two of you will be responsible for everything that goes on with the rodeo, and you will be the point people. She can talk to you more about it, but basically, what you know, I want her to know, and what she knows, I want you to know. So, while you might not work together all day long every day, I definitely want there to be a time in the morning and a time in the evening where you both touch base, discuss what's going on, and pick each other's brains for the best ways to do things. We have…a lot riding on this for the ranch and for all of our futures."

Ezra glanced at Phoebe, then back to Tillman. "It's common knowledge that we were almost in the black. My brother had been able to get a large sum of money and things were looking really good. But we loaded up two pots of finished calves, high dollar beef, and there was an accident."

Tillman flinched. Accidents involving animals were never pretty.

"A car wasn't paying attention and moved to the left lane, hitting the first truck right on the steer tire, causing the tire to blow and that driver to lose control. He ended up upside down in the ditch. The second driver had to careen off the road to avoid hitting the car, and he ended up in the ditch as well."

"And the woman had about $30K worth of insurance, I'd bet, which would not even pay for the clean up." Tillman had driven truck for a while and knew exactly how these things went down. "And your underinsured on the truck policy was probably enough to replace one rig, if that."

"Exactly. And we ate seventy-two beef at about five grand a head. Most of them were killed in the accident, but it turns my stomach even now to think of the ones that weren't." Ezra sighed. "It turns my stomach to think of the money that was lost as well. But that's farming. We're counting on the rodeo to bring in what we lost."

Ezra didn't have to say anything more. If the rodeo wasn't a success, Tillman would be looking for a new job. As would everyone else on the ranch.

He wouldn't wish losing a ranch on anyone. Having to sell his spread had been the second hardest thing he'd ever done. Having to give up full-time access to his children had been the first. It felt like they'd taken part of him with them when they'd ridden away with their mother, her boyfriend driving the car.

With everything in him, he had wanted to go after her, take his kids out of the back of the car, and keep them next to him, but the law was the law, and the judge had ruled against him. Rightly so since he had no house and, at the time, no job.

He needed to stop thinking about her. Being back on a ranch had brought all the feelings back. Where he would be with his, all the work that he had put into building something for his family, and having it yanked away from him.

He wanted to sigh in disgust. He wanted to stay away from women, and now, he had just been slapped in the face by the fact that he was going to have to spend, if not every day all day with another woman, at least a morning and evening appointment with her.

"Phoebe has noted all of our thoughts and ideas about the rodeo, and she also has the budget and knows exactly what the two of you can spend before we have to discuss it with the family." Ezra lifted a shoulder and looked a little sheepish for the first time. "I wish it was more. And if this is a success, it will be more next year, but for this year, we're going to have to do it on a shoestring budget. I'm sorry."

"No problem. Sometimes it doesn't take money, but just a little bit of elbow grease and some ingenuity to make things work. That's what we'll do this year. I will do it to the best of my ability." Tillman could say that confidently. He didn't go into a job thinking he was going to do anything less than his best, and with so much riding on this, he absolutely wasn't going to do anything less than his best for his good friend and the person who had seen him when he was down and held out a hand to help him up rather than kick him as he walked by.

He had been surprised at the people who had done that.

"All right then, I have some other things I need to do, so Phoebe will show you where you're going to stay and talk about what goes on at the ranch. If you have any questions, she can answer them as well as I can, and she has as much authority as I do."

"But if there's ever a disagreement, I always bow to what Ezra says." These words were soft, and she said them with a smile, but they were firm as well.

For some reason, that made Tillman want to lean toward her. The fact that Ezra was content to allow her to have as much authority and say in everything that he did, but she insisted on giving him the last say. It was the exact opposite of what he would expect out in the world. A Christian principle that she had firmly, but quietly, insisted she adhered to. That she would put others ahead of herself.

Ezra smiled. "She's not hard to get along with." He gave her an affectionate squeeze with his arm around her shoulders, and she looked up at him with just as much admiration in her eyes.

It was just a second, and then Ezra nodded at Tillman and walked into the house.

"I had no idea when I ran into you this morning who you were. I'm sorry."

"Yeah. No problem." Maybe when he was younger, the next words wouldn't have come out of his mouth, but as he got older, he'd learned that sometimes it was better to face things head-on. "Is it a regular thing that you end up in jail? Will I be bailing you out?"

Her eyes got wide and her mouth dropped, and then she closed her eyes and laughed, shaking her head.

"You made the obvious assumption, but it's not the accurate one." She laughed again. "Come on. Let's walk toward the bunkhouse. I'll show you where you're going to stay, and I'll explain exactly what was going on."

"All right," he said, still not entirely sure what would have caused that reaction. Why were they laughing about incarceration? "My stuff is still in my truck."

"All right," she said, striding off the porch and waiting for him to catch up before walking beside him to his pickup.

He didn't have a whole lot, just a few changes of clothes and his saddle and tack in the back.

"We can leave your tack there for now. I'll show you where we can hang it later. It'll probably be easier to just drive your truck to the shed rather than walking."

He jerked his head but didn't say anything as they walked to the bunkhouse, him carrying his two duffels and her with his backpack slung over her shoulder, which contained his comb, toothbrush, razor, and his Bible, so it wasn't very heavy.

"There is a girl who lives with us. Her parents got divorced, and they've been struggling. They wanted her to go somewhere where she wasn't going to be subjected to the fighting and squabbling that went on at their house. It degenerated from there into affairs and that type of thing, and…Mina is staying with us indefinitely."

"All right," he said, trying not to cringe when he heard about the divorce and the squabbling and the fighting. That had been his house for a while. And he hated it. He wasn't a squabbling and fighting kind of guy. But Nicole had yelled at him, screamed at him more like it, more than once that he was a terrible communicator, he wouldn't talk to her, and he didn't give her time to say what she needed to say. He tried to be better, but it had usually degenerated into an argument, because what she had to say was so far away from the truth that he couldn't let it go.

He'd like to think that if he could go back and do it over again, he'd be more patient, more considerate, a better husband somehow, but…he wasn't sure whether that was true.

"She goes to school at the local high school. It's not very big, but she's involved in all the activities she can be. She's just that type of girl. Outgoing, friendly, and social."

"I see."

"Well, one of the things that she was doing for her class was to raise money for a good cause, and that was by getting people to stay overnight at the jail, basically like a lock-in, only it was a fundraiser, where people donate money in order to have someone stay in jail all night. Just a fun twist on the normal fundraisers."

Chapter 4

"Oh. I see." The light had come on for Tillman. "You weren't in jail because you had done anything wrong. You were in jail for a fundraiser for your...friend who lives here on the ranch."

Man, he felt like an idiot. He had judged Phoebe, intentionally or no, based on where he'd seen her, and even went so far as to think that she might have been tipsy.

"Yeah. That was my first time in jail. Hopefully it will be my last too, although I think there were a few people who really enjoyed seeing me there and who would donate a lot of money to the cause."

"You have enemies?"

"More like friends who have a twisted sense of humor," Phoebe said with a laugh, not explaining any further. But she didn't really need to. He had friends like that. Good friends, friends who knew him so well that they knew that having him do something out of character, something that would make him uncomfortable, would probably be good for him.

"Sometimes friends can be a real pain in the butt," he said, but while his voice sounded a little gruff, there was affection in it, which he intended.

"Yeah. But you wouldn't trade them for the world, and sometimes I'm one of those pain-in-the-butt friends to my friends."

He doubted that. She didn't look like she had the ability to tease in her. She just looked sweet and…way too nice. Too nice for her own good. Too nice to work on a ranch. Too nice to be in the same world with people like Nicole.

No. Nicole had gotten him under her spell to begin with. He had fallen for that sweet, pretty face and her big blue eyes when they batted up at him, and her silky blonde hair that fell in shimmering waves over her shoulders. The curve of her hip, the turn of her ankle, and all of the other things that he admired about her had totally blinded him to her true character. He wasn't going to be that ridiculously stupid again.

Never again.

"I'm sorry I jumped to the wrong conclusion," he said, remembering that Nicole had told him that he needed to learn to apologize, instead of yelling at her and trying to defend himself.

At the time, he thought that she needed to take some of her own advice, because she never apologized, and she would say it was because she was never wrong.

He disagreed. But he couldn't change her, he could only change himself, and she was right. He didn't like to apologize. He found, in the short time since she'd said that, that it was easier to apologize right away than it was to go back and dig up old bones. He'd rather put things to bed and let them stay there.

"It's okay. It's perfectly acceptable. I would have done the same thing if I would have met someone coming out of the jail. I would just assume that they were there because of something they'd done wrong and probably even made judgments about their character because of that."

"Guilty. I assumed you were tipsy when you ran into me."

She laughed. "Well, I've never been accused of being drunk before, but I am clumsy. I guess I should just warn you now. I would love to be one of those tall, graceful kind of people, but unfortunately, I never outgrew the tall, gangly stage, where you seem like you're more elbows and knees and feet that get in the way than anything else."

He disagreed. She walked gracefully, matching his stride. There weren't too many women who he didn't have to slow his walk down for so they could keep up, but Phoebe matched him perfectly.

Which did not matter. Not in the slightest.

"All right. This is the bunkhouse. The guests stay on the other side. We put a wall up so that if we had any hired help, they could stay here. A couple of my brothers choose to stay here as well." She paused. "We only have family working on the ranch, except Stonewall. He was friends with our family, and with my sister Johanna in particular, and he moved with us when we moved from Wyoming."

"Wow. He must've really liked you guys to move that far."

Phoebe looked around, and then she lowered her voice. "I think he had some ulterior motives, but he really did grow up with us. He's worked on our ranch, first for my dad, when he was even younger than a teenager, and goodness, he's done as much work here as any of us have. He certainly deserves to move wherever we do."

Deserves. Like just because he acted like he was a part of the family he deserved to be treated like it. That was kind of a novel idea too. But after knowing Ezra in college, he knew the Clyborne family wasn't a typical family. First of all, there were twelve kids in their family. No one had a family like that anymore. In fact, it was almost impossible to. Laws were certainly not geared toward making life easy for families with more than two or three kids.

She opened the door to the bunkhouse and led him down a hallway with the occasional door off to the right.

"This used to be all one big room, but we figured that folks would want a little room for privacy. So, there isn't much to the bedrooms, just a single bed, a dresser and mirror, and a chair and lamp. An end table as well. We have a rack for you to hang up a few clothes, but not enough room to hang many."

She walked to the end of the hall and opened up the last door on the right.

"They're all the same, except for this one which is slightly bigger. My brother just moved out of it, and when Ezra heard you were coming, he asked me to get this one ready for you."

If it was slightly bigger than the other ones, Tillman couldn't imagine how small they must be.

"He said you were pretty tall and could use the extra space." Phoebe had a little bit of humor in her voice, and she had been talking like they were friends, even though they had just met each other that morning. There was just a casual, friendly-type demeanor to her that he found both attractive and off putting.

He didn't want anyone to know him that well. He didn't want to have new friends. He didn't want to open up his heart or his life or his soul again. He wanted to close it off and protect it. That wasn't necessarily a deliberate decision that he had made, but it was something he wanted to do nonetheless.

"This will be just fine," he said, although he hadn't been asked. It wasn't like he was going to get offered anything else. His only other choice would be to quit the job and find a different job. That wasn't going to happen, so whatever they gave him, whether a room like this, or a spot in the barn under a leaky roof, or told him to go find his own lodging somewhere else, he would do it.

Farms and ranches, especially family farms and ranches, were going under at an alarming pace. He could work for a big corporation, and he might have to at some point, but as long as he could choose to work for a small ranch, the kind that he wanted for himself, he would do it. No matter the hardship.

"The other reason that Ezra wanted you to have this room is because of this." Phoebe had walked over and opened a door on the left-hand side of the room. "We had a little bit of extra room when we were laying things out and putting in the plans for the rooms, and we ended up with two small rooms on this side."

She stepped back so he could see.

"Originally we were going to make them into bathrooms, but we put beds in them and kinda thought that maybe if our guests had a family that needed to have some privacy for some reason, someone who was physically disabled…or something. We just…didn't really know. But maybe it was God. He knew you'd be here, and you'd have your kids staying at some point. So, this room has two bedrooms off it, just small rooms with beds and nothing else, where your kids can stay when they come to visit."

So she knew about his children. Probably because of Ezra. It unsettled him a little to know that she knew something he hadn't told her, that she'd been talking about him when he wasn't around.

He didn't know what Ezra thought, didn't know what Ezra would have told her, other than he'd never heard Ezra say an unkind word about anyone, so he didn't think that Ezra would all of a sudden have gone out of character and started talking badly about him.

For some reason, that was important to him. He wanted Phoebe to think the best of him.

Not that he cared. Not that there was going to be anything between them, not for any reason like that, just…he already thought highly of her, and he wanted her feelings about him to be mutual, he supposed.

Whatever it was, he tried to shake it off. But he couldn't shake off his gratitude. This would go a long way toward what he wanted at his next court date. To get his children for the summer. If Nicole was going to have them the whole school year, it was only fair that he got them for the summer.

He wasn't sure how he was going to pull that off, since he figured they would be sharing whatever accommodations he had, which…he had thought might be a communal room with all of the hands—one room with beds strewn along the walls like a person might find at a summer camp for kids. Those were the accommodations he had before.

This was better than what he had dared to hope for.

Hopefully the judge would see it that way too.

"I really appreciate your consideration. Custody has been…a battle. I suppose that's why people talk about battling for custody. But this might actually help me in my quest."

"I can't imagine being separated from my children." Phoebe lifted her shoulder. "I was never blessed with children or a husband, but I raised my younger siblings as my own, and seeing them go off to college just tore my heart out. Even though I knew it was for the best, that they were doing what they needed to do with their lives, it was hard. I can't imagine having them taken from me when they were younger."

So she'd never married. And if she was just a little bit younger than Ezra, that meant she was just a little younger than him. Maybe thirty-six or thirty-seven. Since he was knocking hard on forty at thirty-eight.

"Yeah," he said, not saying anything more.

The rooms were very simple and small, as Phoebe had said. Just a bed and a small nightstand with a lamp on it. That was it. There was a small area where his door opened, with the door to the right and then a door to the left. Neither of the rooms had windows.

Maybe, he'd be able to spend some nights under the stars with his kids. Although, that wasn't something he was going to ask about today. He didn't even know if he was going to be able to get his kids here. He was pretty much at Nicole's mercy, since he was allowed to visit at her house, but he was not allowed to take the children with him overnight. At the time the judge had issued that order, he hadn't had a home or a job.

His new court date should hopefully show that he had both and would hopefully get him more time with his kids.

"If you need some time to unpack, that's fine, just say so," Phoebe said as they closed the door and she walked to the opening of his room. Like she didn't want to stand in his room with him. He hadn't seen her looking uncomfortable at all, but just the way her hands moved at her waist, like she didn't know where to put them until she got to the door, made him think that either being in the room with him made her uncomfortable or being alone with him? He wasn't sure. Something had made her feel a little antsy though. It wasn't hard to see that at least.

"I don't need any time. I'll deal with this when I get off tonight. I was supposed to start today, and I intend to put in a full day's work."

She nodded, smiling, like she had expected it. "All right. Let's go back and get your saddle, and if you don't mind driving your pickup, I'll ride along with you and show you where we keep the horses and tack."

"All right. I don't mind."

She led him back through the hall. It was dark and narrow, but he understood why—to give the rooms as much space as possible.

"You do share a bathroom, and that's here," she said, pointing to the last door on the left as they walked out. "We cook all the meals, including breakfast. Typically, we pack a lunch, where you have a sandwich to take with you or can come back to the ranch and grab it, and a full supper as well. It depends on how busy everyone is as to whether the food is hot or cold. In harvest season or during days that we're working the cattle, food is scarce and cold, typically. Although, with Alaska here, that's Ezra's wife—"

"I met her," he interjected, when she had a bit of a question in her voice.

She nodded, acknowledging his words. "She does a lot better job of just staying in the house and making sure people eat. I was always supposed to be cooking, but then someone would need me outside, and I'd go, and we'd end up eating the bits and pieces that I could scratch together when I was done working. As I got better at it, I planned for those times and made meals that involved the crockpot in the morning and food ready for a big lunch, then we'd have leftovers for supper."

"All right," he said, not bothering to say that anything that she made would be better than what he made for himself. He could cook; it wasn't rocket science, but he never put a lot of effort into it. He'd rather be out doing something than spending time in the kitchen, because once a person cooked, there was the cleanup to do as well. So, sandwiches were pretty much what he'd subsided on, along with canned soup, and anything that was easy. Anything that could be made in the microwave in five minutes or less.

He had a feeling he'd be eating better here than he ever had in his life before. And somehow, with that thought, came another. There would be a lot of things he would be doing here that would be better than they'd ever been in his life before.

Chapter 5

Phoebe walked beside Tillman, thankful that she wasn't squirming with embarrassment anymore. He had thought she had been in jail. Of course, that was the logical thing to think when he met her on the steps of the jail for the first time, having no idea who she was. Still, she supposed she just thought that people looked at her and knew that she wasn't that type of person. That showed a level of delusion that, at thirty-six years old, she probably should have outgrown at least a couple of decades before.

Of course, people couldn't look at her and tell anything about her character or her integrity or anything.

And there were plenty of good people who made mistakes and ended up in places they would never have expected to end up.

Maybe she was one of those people, in a way. Looking back over her life, there wasn't much she would change, including taking care of her siblings after her parents died. But that had led to the fact that she hadn't exactly been out where she could meet men and find someone to share her life with. She had children to take care of, siblings to raise, school to do, ranch work to do, and other than grocery shopping and church, and various homeschool activities, she never left the ranch.

It made her a little bit sad now, especially since her younger siblings had grown up and left. Some of them had come back, but Lois was talking like she might never come back, and it made Phoebe sad. She loved the idea of the whole family living and working on the ranch, seeing each other on a daily basis, living life together, doing their very best to make their little corner of the earth a place that shone for Jesus every day.

Hundreds of years ago, and any time prior to that, it was totally normal for children to grow up and stay close to the place where they had been born. It was only in the last century or so that kids had looked at where they came from and felt like they needed to spread their wings and go somewhere else.

Phoebe knew it was a very old-fashioned idea, but she longed for the time where family stayed together.

Of course, there were the families in the 1800s who traveled west, left their parents, their siblings, and everything they knew to take their kids and head toward the promise of a better life.

So maybe that idea was older than what she gave it credit for.

She just never had that urge.

"That building is where we eat. It also has some rooms in it for families who stay at our dude ranch. It has a big room with tables where we serve the meals. We still cook at the house, but one of the improvements that we'd like to make eventually is to add a kitchen area to that building so we don't have to carry the food from the house across the yard. It's not far, but still."

"I understand. No one likes cold food."

"Exactly," she said. Although, she loved cooking in the big house. It wouldn't be quite the same if she were cooking in a place where it didn't feel like family lived there. An industrial-type kitchen. Although it would be convenient in a lot of ways. Pros and cons. Everything had them. There was never a decision that she made that was all pros and no cons.

And of course, every dark place had its beam of sunlight. It was like God knew humans couldn't stand to not be encouraged, that they needed that little spark of light.

God was good, all the time, and He always sent the light. Sometimes it was just harder to see than others.

Beside her, Tillman strode, silent, although not afraid to talk when it was his turn. He had made several statements without her prompting, which encouraged her that maybe they would be able to communicate after all.

Ezra had described Tillman as quiet to the point of having to pry words out of him at times. It would be very difficult to put a rodeo together with someone who was unable to communicate with her.

She could hardly keep accurate, detailed notes and keep things organized if she didn't know what was going on.

But she hadn't been expecting this…feeling that seemed to be passing between the two of them. She felt it on the steps of the jail. Maybe it was what made her trip the second time. Just something odd about being in his presence. Something unsettling.

It wasn't a bad thing, because she admired him. Not only was he appealing, although maybe not quite handsome. With the stubble on his jaw, the serious look in his eyes that were shaded by the brim of his cowboy hat, the loose, casual way he held himself, not slouching but not walking around with his chest puffed out like a peacock either. She'd never been attracted to conceited, arrogant know-it-alls.

Typically, she loved a man with a sense of humor, and Tillman hadn't made her laugh, but this was his first day on the job, and a normal person would be nervous, although he did not seem the slightest bit bothered. He hadn't needed a break and didn't want to rest.

"If you ever miss lunch for any reason, if you're out working and don't make it in, typically the leftovers are in the fridge at the big house, and Alaska is almost always there. But if she's not, right there is the back door, where you can go in and help yourself to anything in the fridge."

"I probably won't do that."

"A lot of times, we assume that of the newcomers and take their food out to them. My brothers have no such reluctance, and if you're working with one of them, they'll drag you in by your ear most likely. Not too much gets between them and their food."

"I think that's typical for the male gender."

"It seems to be typical for the female gender too, or maybe I'm just an anomaly."

"You don't look like you have a problem pushing away from the table."

It wasn't personal, not really. But he was commenting on the way she looked.

She didn't take it in any way other than how she felt he meant it—a casual comment made in conversation that meant nothing.

"My dad was tall and thin. My mom was short and curvy. Well, not short, but shorter than Dad. It seems like us kids either got his frame or hers. I ended up with his, which most of the time is okay."

But it had narrowed down her dating pool if she wanted to be with someone who was taller than she was. Not that she dated a lot, since her family didn't really encourage that. But it had narrowed down the people that she allowed herself to be interested in. She didn't really want to look down on her husband. And she assumed that her husband wouldn't want to have to look up to her. Although, she'd seen couples like that and always wondered if maybe she'd fall in love and it wouldn't matter how tall the man was.

Or maybe she should say that God would put the perfect man in front of her, and she hoped she was able to get past how tall he was to see that he was the one for her.

She was tempted to ask Tillman which side of the family he took after, since that seemed to be the way the conversation was going, but Ezra said that he never talked about his past and he hadn't had a very happy childhood.

It seemed like someone like him should have had a happy marriage, but that hadn't happened for him either. Some people just seemed to get all the bad breaks.

They made it to his truck, and she gave him directions to the pole building where they had horse stalls and kept their tack.

As she led him in, she pointed out some of their ranch horses, although most of them were out in the pasture. Only the ones that needed some special care were inside. Most of the stalls were empty.

"Any open hook on this wall can be yours. The other wall is where we keep the saddles that we use for guests. And occasionally we have a guest who brings their own saddle, and it goes on that wall as well. When something is hanging here, we know it belongs to a specific person, and no one else touches it."

"Good to know. I'm kind of attached to my saddle."

"I can't believe you only have one."

"I lost all my other ones in the divorce."

Right.

He said it so flatly, so unemotionally, that she knew there was a whole well of deep, seething emotion underneath it. But she didn't want to go there. She couldn't imagine going through what he had gone through, losing his ranch, and it would have to have meant more to him than it would to her.

At least if she lost her ranch, she'd still have her family. But they worked so hard after their parents died to keep the ranch so their family could stay together. That had been the two main things in her life, ranch and family.

And Tillman lost them both.

He hung up his saddle, put his bridle on a peg as well, and she led him through a short tour of the barn, showing where the feed was and that type of thing.

As they walked through the other end of the barn, they came out in the bright sunlight, next to several high-top tables with two chairs at each of them.

"This is a nice place to sit. Typically the guests don't go back here, and it's relatively quiet." She paused. "If you don't mind, I was hoping we could sit at one of these tables and kind of hash out how we're going to work things. We have a big job ahead of us, and I suppose we ought to talk about the burden of responsibility and everything."

"We can, although Ezra told me that I would be doing everything that had to do with actual knowledge of the rodeo, and you would be keeping things organized and making sure the details were taken care of."

"Yes. That's exactly right. But I just wanted to make sure that you understood that while you and I are working together, and I'm technically in charge, if you need any time off, I'm the one who will approve that. I know you're on salary, but I don't think that making sure that you put in a sufficient number of hours every week is going to be an issue."

"I really don't know anything else other than getting up in the morning and going to work, and coming in at dark to go to bed."

"That's what I thought. That's what Ezra said, and I wasn't worried about that. But I think that since you're the one with the knowledge of what we need to do, you're the one that should be technically in charge. Does that make sense?"

His brows furrowed, and then he said, "Maybe you're right. Maybe we ought to sit down and talk about this."

"Thanks." She appreciated that he could shift gears, see that he wasn't seeing the whole picture, and admit that maybe her idea had been right to begin with.

They settled at the table, and she pulled her phone out.

"If you don't mind, I'll just record what we're saying, and then later tonight, I'll take some notes, make a few spreadsheets, and do whatever else I think I need to do in order to get started with the organization end."

"I don't mind at all, and that's actually a pretty good idea." He sounded slightly surprised that she was getting into her job immediately.

"So I just told you that I would like for you to be in charge. I mean, not of me, but of the project. If that's what we can call it."

"Sure. We're putting on a rodeo. That's a big project."

"And that's the end goal. But there are lots of little steps to get to that end goal. I can keep track of the little steps, check off the things that we've done, but you are the one that knows, for instance, what type of pen we would need if we were going to do barrel racing, for example. What kind of layout we have to have set up for that, and whether we can do calf roping in the same area."

"I haven't seen all the buildings yet, but so far, I haven't seen anything that's going to work for those types of things. Ezra told me that we are on a shoestring budget, so I think the best thing to do is probably use a paddock that we have that's about the right size. We'll put up temporary bleachers, and we'll make sure that the ground is appropriately prepared, mostly to keep the horses from hurting themselves in whatever aspect they're being used. There is a certain way the ground should feel. It definitely should not be hard, and it shouldn't be soft either, because a horse can catch a hoof and pull a tendon or break a leg. I've seen it happen."

"Oh, that's terrible," Phoebe said and couldn't contain her shiver. She had seen several horses put down, and it was never an easy thing. She'd seen grown cowboys crying over their horses, and she couldn't blame them. When they worked so hard for a person, it was heartbreaking to know that there was nothing someone could do to help them get better. It was also terrible to see them in distress, fear, and pain.

"So… I'd like to know exactly what the budget is, and then I think we need to have a list of all the things you think you're going to need, because I assume you're going to have food, possibly even vendor booths set up, and that's going to take money. I don't want to spend more than what I have, but I also don't want to cut corners that don't need to be cut."

She winced a little when he said cut corners. All her life, she'd been taught that it was terrible to cut corners, but when it came to finances, sometimes it was necessary.

They talked for a while, and Tillman was all business. His knowledge of the rodeo far exceeded hers, and maybe she shouldn't have been impressed. Maybe anyone with a rudimentary knowledge of rodeo knew what he knew, but she was impressed nonetheless.

They'd been talking for a while when Phoebe's stomach growled. She looked down at her phone to catch the time, and she gasped when she realized that two hours had gone by.

"Wow. You must be starving. I'm so sorry, I didn't realize that we'd been sitting here so long."

She felt like they had gotten an awful lot accomplished. They had some ground rules laid, and Tillman had obviously been thinking hard about it, because he knew exactly what he wanted, and he was able to rattle off a list of the things that he couldn't do without, things that he wanted but if they absolutely couldn't afford it, he could live without, and then things that would be nice to have if they had some extra money.

She hadn't been nearly that organized. She didn't have any clue about how much food she should budget for, or whether they should build booths for people or just rent tables, and how much that would cost.

"This is great to start with. I should be able to have some things set up by this evening, if we want to meet again today and go over things."

"Ezra said we would be meeting morning and evening, and I thought that might be a little much, but to get started with, we can assume the evening meeting is to talk about what we got accomplished that day, and the morning meeting will be for discussion about what we're going to do."

"Yes. That's exactly what I thought. We also need to set a date for the rodeo, and…we need to set your schedule as well."

She knew he wanted to say something different than what he was actually going to say, she could tell from the reluctance on his face and the way his folded hands tightened and his thumb twitched in agitation.

"I have to have a day off next week. I have a date for revisiting our custody agreement. Now that I have a job and a place to stay, and thanks to you and Ezra, I have a place for my kids. I'm hoping to get them for the summer."

"That's fine," she said immediately. She wasn't sure if his reluctance was a fear that they would think that he wouldn't be able to do his job if he had his children with him or something else.

"Do you know how old they are?" he asked, his eyes narrowing, like he thought she might have been speaking too soon.

"Ezra told me that you were honest and you had character. He said that you are quiet, and I worried a little that I wouldn't be able to have a discussion with you like we just had this morning. That worry is alleviated. He also said that you didn't have the best childhood, and that you'd had a tough break with your marriage, nasty divorce, and you're hoping to be able to see your children more. That's all I know about you."

There. She laid it on the table. She didn't see any point in keeping things back when putting them out would make everything a little more clear for everyone.

He nodded, like he appreciated the fact that she wasn't pulling any punches. "My kids are seven and nine."

"All right. I guess I assumed that they were not toddlers anymore, but I could have been wrong about that. Still, we'd figure something out. This is a family operation. You and Stonewall are the only two people who aren't married to a sibling or blood relations who work here."

"I appreciate that. But there won't be any other children for me." That was said with a finality that Phoebe didn't even think about arguing with. "My arbitration date is next Tuesday. It's a six-hour drive there, which I can do Monday evening after I get off work. The meeting is at eleven AM, and I doubt it will last more than an hour. I'll be back by Tuesday night, but I'll need the whole day on Tuesday off."

"Done." Phoebe didn't hesitate. "If you do get your children, and you need time to…take them somewhere, the dentist, the doctor, on a picnic, that time is yours. Family is more important than anything."

"More important than even keeping the ranch solvent?"

"If I thought that was going to be a problem with you, I might not say it quite the way I am, but yeah. Your family is more important. Take the time you need to be with them."

He stared at her, and not for the first time, she wondered what he was thinking. It was obvious something was going on in his head, but it was also obvious that she was never going to find out what it was.

Maybe he was surprised that she was putting family ahead of financial security, but in her experience, strong family meant financial security. Of course, his experience was completely different.

Not for the first time, she wondered what his experience had been. How had his family life not been good, according to Ezra? Phoebe knew she could probably ask Ezra, and while he wouldn't tell her any details that he felt were confidential, he would tell her general things that everyone knew.

Had Tillman grown up in a single-parent home? Had he gone through a nasty divorce as a child? Had neither of his parents wanted him? Surely if he had lost both of his parents, Ezra would have told her, because that would have been something she and Tillman could have bonded over. She knew what it was like to lose her parents, suddenly and with no chance to say goodbye.

Regardless, it probably wasn't going to change anything. He was keeping a very professional distance from her, and while she wouldn't have minded being on friendlier terms, terms where she felt comfortable joking and laughing and talking about personal things, she supposed it was for the best. They would get more work done, and be more focused on their jobs, if they were less focused on the relationship between the two of them.

"Let's go over and get some lunch, and I'll show you around the rest of the buildings. We do have some lumber left over from some building projects, and you're welcome to use any of that."

"Did you guys just put these buildings up?" he asked as she stood up from her chair, and he waited for her before they set off to the big house together.

"Most of them were up when we bought the place. We put the pole building up for the horses and tack, but most of the buildings just needed some maintenance done to them, and we were able to use them. The barn where we keep the hay is the oldest building, and we almost tore it down. If we would have had more money, we would have. The wiring in it is spotty, and at least once or twice a week, something blows a breaker there."

"Doesn't sound safe."

"No. We don't let the guests go there. But we wanted to have small bales to feed the horses, and we needed a place to store it. A pole building would have been a lot better and a lot easier, but we have the bundles of hay stacked on the barn floor and in the loft areas."

"I'm happy you said bundles. When you said small bales, I thought maybe I was going to be getting roped into baling hay, and while I've done it before, it's hard work."

"It sure is. But no, we have all the equipment to make bundles. That all came from Wyoming. We haven't purchased anything new in a while, just trying to get things off the ground here."

"There's a lot of pressure, since it has to support twelve people."

"Yeah. Our two younger siblings are still in college, and they're paying their own way, with a few scholarships, but it's still a lot of people for one ranch to support. That's why we have so many different things we're working on."

"It's smart to branch out."

He didn't say anything more, and they walked together to the kitchen, where she showed him how to go in the back door, where the refrigerator was, and she showed him the stash of sandwiches that had already been put there for the rest of the day.

"I know it feels a little bit weird to just walk into someone's house and grab stuff out of the refrigerator, but we would really rather you do that than work hungry. We're not trying to starve anyone. And we know with the accommodations that you have that you don't exactly have the ability to go home and cook for yourself. If that were different, it'd be a completely different story."

"Yeah. I see."

He didn't sound like he had been convinced of anything, and she made a mental note to make sure that she kept an eye on him and made sure he was eating. She wouldn't want to walk into someone's house and just get in the refrigerator, either. Maybe after he worked there for a while, he would feel more comfortable. She hoped so.

But for the time being, he already was slim and didn't look like he had any weight to lose. She did not want him skipping meals.

The sandwiches were labeled, and she noted that he took two ham and cheese.

"They don't put condiments on them, but they're right there in the refrigerator door."

He jerked his head, grabbing the mustard.

She took a turkey sandwich out and the mayonnaise. She also grabbed a bag of onions and lettuce.

"Sometimes we have tomato slices as well, but anything that's in these bags are things that we can put on our sandwiches. Most of the time, most of the guys aren't interested in putting any kind of vegetable on, but I really like lettuce and onion on mine."

"I'll take some onions too," he said calmly as he stood beside her at the counter while she grabbed two paper plates and set her sandwich on one, getting a knife and spreading the mayonnaise on it and pulling some onions and lettuce out of the bags to stick on her sandwich as well.

"Sometimes I'm in a hurry and I don't bother to do this, but even though I don't think there's too much nutritional value in lettuce and onions, it still makes me feel like I'm getting my vegetables for the day if I do that. And it soothes some of my guilt for putting mayonnaise on it."

"Mayonnaise is in a food group all its own," Tillman said, and for the first time, Phoebe got the idea that he might have been making a joke. Maybe he did have a sense of humor underneath that taciturn personality. She looked forward to finding out.

Chapter 6

"I've been told you're the man I need to talk to about building anything around here." Tillman spoke to Tobias, one of Phoebe's many younger brothers.

One drawback to having a large family was the fact that anyone who came into the family had to figure out everyone else. In the two days that Tillman had been there, he barely figured out names, let alone birth order.

He had a lot of other things to think about and figured that the Clybornes would all agree that was not the most important thing that he needed to be thinking about. Still, he liked to have all the information he could, and he really appreciated getting the details right, but he also knew that sometimes things just took a little bit of time. Eventually he would figure out birth order, but in the meantime, he was just happy to know Tobias's name.

"I don't know who told you that, because everyone around here knows how to wield a hammer and use a drill and a tape measure, even my sisters." Tobias didn't say that like there was anything special about his sisters being able to do it. More like a stranger might not know, or might assume, that they could only work in the kitchen. "But I'm happy to help you with whatever I can."

"Phoebe told me that you would. But I also know that what I want is going to take some time, and you have other jobs you need to pay attention to. Since the first thing we're trying to do is nail down a date, the earliest date possible, but with enough time to get everything ready, for the rodeo. I just thought I would throw out what I needed to get done, and you can give me a ballpark idea of how much time it will take you, including the time that you'll need to be spending on other jobs."

Tobias nodded, even though that hadn't been the most clear explanation Tillman had ever given. He was a little overwhelmed, if he was being honest. This was a much bigger job than what he had anticipated. They had no arena, no bleachers, no stables where horses could be housed, and the only accommodations they had were the ones they used for the dude ranch guests.

Tillman was going to assume that they were hoping a lot of the dude ranch guests would be booking accommodations for the rodeo dates, hence there would be no place to put up people who might drive from a thousand miles away just to participate in the rodeo.

Most of the rodeo folks that he knew had accommodations in their horse trailers and were no strangers to sleeping in those or in the back seats of their pickups. Still, it was always nice when a person could go somewhere and get a shower at the very least.

So that was what he was going to do, since there was no time or money to put up an entire building to house participants. He was just going to focus on toilets and showers. Most likely they would be renting the toilets, but to his knowledge, there was no such thing as shower rentals, and they were going to need to figure something out. Preferably something that would go along with the ranch's long-term plan, so anything they built could eventually be integrated into buildings that they intended to put up when finances allowed.

He really did want to work with the Clybornes, rather than take from them. Of course, the success of the rodeo would be a feather in his cap, but he wasn't just about feathering his cap.

That was a selfish way to live, and he'd been on the receiving end of that more than once in his life. It didn't make him determined to be selfish, it made him determined to be the opposite. Although, he'd seen it have that effect on other people. People who would say, "I'm going to take more from you than you take from me" and that type of thing.

At least he hoped he wasn't like that. Although he couldn't say that he wouldn't take the opportunity to pay his ex-wife back in spades for the pain and suffering she put him through. In fact, he had to stop himself from looking for opportunities to be as unkind to her as she had been to him. The desire was strong.

He showed his plans to Tobias and told him the least amount that he thought that they needed in order to pull this off.

"Of course, we can have a bigger and better rodeo if we rent the fairgrounds at Rockerton. We can also go to any of the neighboring ranches, where they have accommodations, as I understand it. I haven't been out to check, and I don't have any plans on going, because I assumed that we wanted this to be something that took place right here on our ranch property. Sweet View Ranch."

"Yeah. I think that's important. The idea is not always to make money this year, which I hope we do, but also to get something started that will be a moneymaker every year. We can hardly have the first annual Sweet View Ranch rodeo on someone else's spread."

"That's exactly what I was thinking, so that's why I've come up with this list." He hadn't thought Tobias or anyone else would want to do it somewhere else. It was something he hadn't talked to Phoebe about, because they had so many things to go through in their last two meetings.

So help him, he was looking forward to talking to her tonight. He was disappointed that they hadn't gotten to work together today. She had some things she'd already committed to, and told him that he was on his own, after apologizing.

Of course he waved off her apology, and he'd also shoved aside his disappointment. It irritated him more than anything. He didn't want to look forward to seeing some woman. He didn't want her to walk in his view and his whole being light up with excitement and happiness. He didn't want to admire the way her neck curved, to get lost in the blue depths of her eyes, watch as her hair blew in the wind and she shoved it out of her face, fighting the urge to lift his hand up and help her. To have his fingers wrap around hers, to pull her toward him and… Yeah. It was better for him not to be working with Phoebe and for them to work together as little as possible.

"Once I get the materials, I think I can put these things in pretty easily. They're just showers and drains, and it's brown water, not septic, so we should be good just having a drain field. I think we can even make a pad for the job johnnies, that will make things a little easier, and I wanted to cement an area that we can use as seating for when it's wet and muddy out." Tobias spoke softly, as though talking to himself. He narrowed his eyes and tapped his chin as he looked over the rest.

"Can I have a copy of this?" he asked, pointing to the list that Tillman had held in his hand.

Phoebe had actually taken what he had made yesterday and what he had shown her this morning and made six or seven copies of it. She laughed and said that a person could just take a picture on their phone and have it just as easily, but it wasn't as big.

And he appreciated her foresight now as he pulled one of the copies that she made out of his notebook and handed it to Tobias.

"Phoebe said you could take a picture with your phone if you wanted to," he said.

Tobias grinned. "That's a good idea. It'll be a little small, but I'll have the paper to refer to when I need it, and I'll have my phone all the time."

He snapped a pic and thanked Tillman.

"This is a little bigger job than what you were expecting?" Tobias asked as he shoved his phone back in his pocket and folded the piece of paper.

"I can handle it," Tillman said, not wanting to show weakness. Then, because Tobias seemed like the kind of guy who thought about things, he said, "It is going to be the biggest thing I've ever attempted though. I still think as long as we're careful with our expenses, we'll make money no matter what. The thing is, will it be enough?"

Tobias nodded his head. Tillman had no idea of how much was enough. And if Tobias knew, he didn't say.

Tillman figured that was for the best. He didn't want that pressure on his shoulders right now. He had enough going on, and he knew that financial pressure could crush a man. He'd been under it for years, after his marriage. His wife had insisted on spending money they didn't have to make her living accommodations be up to her standards. She had also run up credit card bills he didn't know about and had bought vehicles they couldn't afford.

She didn't have a care in the world, because if they lost the ranch, it actually would make her happier.

He wished he would have seen that before he committed his life to her. In particular, before they had children.

But he supposed that life was a series of learning opportunities. Some people lucked into their marriages. Although he hated to say it that way, it was true. He'd heard people say that they were blessed with the way their marriage turned out, and they hadn't known what they were getting into.

Still, he didn't like to think that life was just luck. In his experience, hard work mattered a lot more, although there was nothing he could have done to save his ranch. No one could have worked harder, longer, more than he had. It was just when someone pulled against a person, fought against them, shot down every good thing that they did, trying to make things fail, a man really didn't have much opportunity to fix anything.

"We go over the finances on a regular basis, and I'll talk to Ezra, but I would say that since you're working here, you have a right to know what they are."

"Not sure I want to."

"Same. It's good to have a grasp, but a man can't live with that kind of pressure all the time. Ezra and I've had several talks about that. He's closer to it than any of us are, but we just have to work as hard as we can and let the Lord give the increase."

"Or take everything away," Tillman said, and despite his preference, there was bitterness in those words.

"Sometimes He has to take away in order to give us something better."

"And you're the expert on that?" He wanted to get along with Tobias. He liked the man and respected him. He could tell from the little bit of time they spent together that Tobias was an awful lot like him, even more so than Ezra, quiet and determined, more interested in showing with his actions what he believed than spouting off a bunch of words that didn't mean anything.

"I thought about it a lot after God took my parents away. Wondered why He would do that. There were twelve of us. We were basically orphans. They were doing a good thing. They were living for God, their lives reflected Jesus, and they drew people to them. Lives were changed because they interacted with my parents. And I didn't understand how God's kingdom could be furthered by taking that away. How any of our lives would be better. As for me, I got a little angry."

"Rightfully so. No one should lose their parents like that."

"But I wouldn't be the man I am if I hadn't had to man up at that point. You know? There were a lot of things that fell on our shoulders, a lot of work we had to do, a lot of things we had to walk through, and I had to make the decision as to whether I was going to fall apart or whether I was going to draw closer to the Lord. I have a better relationship with God today because I lost my parents fifteen years ago. It was a hard loss, but God gave me something better. A relationship with Him. Up until that point, I had just kinda been thinking that because I was part of my family, God and I were good. I didn't really have a deep relationship with Him. Not like I do now."

Tillman nodded, but he didn't have a lot to say. He had a better relationship with the Lord before his divorce. After it, things had gone sideways. Or even backward.

But the idea of taking something bad and using it for good, or as Tobias had said, when God took something away, He wanted to fill it with something better. Maybe Tillman was keeping himself in a position where God couldn't fill him with something better because Tillman was in the way.

He knew his attitude hadn't been the best, he knew he was fighting bitterness, he knew he pretty much hated his ex and resented her.

But he didn't know how to get out of any of that. Couldn't change it, and he felt he was justified in his feelings. Still thought he was.

"I'm not judging you, I'm not saying anything. Other than, it's up to you. It's also up to you as to whether you want to be included in the family meetings, but if you do, I think you deserve to be."

"If you guys let me, I'll be there."

Tobias nodded, and they walked along, with Tobias pointing out where he thought Tillman might be best served to use areas for parking and to put up a vendor area. They chatted for a while more, and Tillman walked away with a greater appreciation for Tobias and his calm, steady influence. He didn't preach, and he didn't make Tillman feel bad. Other than maybe convicting Tillman that he wasn't doing everything that he could be. Not in his spiritual life.

He prided himself for working hard physically, but that wasn't the only area of a man's life. And it was kind of silly to be strong in one area and completely weak and lacking in another. It would be like having a strong right arm and a left arm that was withered and useless. He didn't want that to be the way he was as a man.

He wasn't sure exactly what he needed to do to fix the issue. His wife wasn't interested in reconciling, and a man can only do so much himself.

He shook his head as he walked away. If God wanted him to change, He was going to have to show him how.

Chapter 7

"She's so sweet. And I'm so glad you were able to give all of her puppies away," Phoebe said, straightening from where she had knelt down to pet Grace, Ryland's dog.

Ryland and Lucas had gotten married just two months or so before, and Ryland had become a regular on the farm even though they still lived in town, in her small apartment by the library. They were waiting for the finances of the ranch to turn around so they would have money to build a house. In the meantime, they didn't seem unhappy with the way things had turned out. In fact, if Phoebe had any say, she would say Lucas had never been happier.

It made her heart swell to see the light of joy and excitement in her siblings' eyes. To see them fall in love with good people and start families of their own. Ryland was definitely a dear. And Phoebe was happy for the time that she'd gotten to spend with her and to get to know her better.

"I'm thrilled that they all seemed to go to really good homes. All three of their new owners have sent me pictures, and they've stayed in touch. I hope that continues, because it was a lot harder than what I realized it was going to be to allow the puppies to go to their new homes. I mean, I know we couldn't keep them all, but I wanted to."

"I wasn't even as close to them as you are, and I wanted to keep them too. They all had their different personalities, and they were all sweet and cute and cuddly."

Ryland chatted a bit more before she walked away, toward the barn where Lucas was working, with Grace following on her heels.

Phoebe turned, heading toward the garden. They had a few early vegetables in, and there were never enough hands to help with the work there. Not that she had a whole lot of time to spare, but she had told Priscilla that she would spend an hour in the garden with her today, and she needed to keep her word. Not to mention, she knew her twin was going through a hard time, and she wanted to be there for her, although she really wasn't sure of what she could do, other than to provide a listening ear and compassion.

Priscilla was already in the garden, kneeling down, weeding the onions.

Phoebe went over to the other side of the row so they could face each other, and she knelt down directly opposite Priscilla. Priscilla had been weeding the entire row up until that point, and now, they'd done it long enough that they would automatically both just weed half of the row. It would go faster, and they could stay together and talk.

Back when they were kids, there would be the expected arguments about where the middle of the row was, and there would be weeds left in the row, as each of them refused to pull anything that might possibly be on the other person's side.

Phoebe didn't know how her parents put up with those kinds of arguments, but they were resolved, all the weeds were out, and she and Priscilla had grown up as each other's best friend.

There was no one else in the world she loved more, and no one else in the world who knew her better. Even though they had ten other siblings, there was a special bond between the two of them. Whether it was because they were twins, or whether it was just because they were the same age and had spent so much time together, Phoebe didn't really know. She didn't care either, she just knew she loved her twin and would do anything for her.

"You've been spending a lot of time here. There are hardly any weeds anywhere," Phoebe said as a few minutes passed without them doing more than saying hello.

"It's the best place to think." Priscilla sounded especially despondent, and Phoebe's heart hurt with each beat in her chest.

"I agree. It's nice to keep your hands busy with mindless tasks while you think about what you can do, but not ruminate, you know?"

"I've done my share of ruminating," Priscilla said, still sounding sad but a little bit of humor in her voice as well.

"I think we all have. But it can eat us up inside."

"I know."

Phoebe pulled several more weeds out, careful not to disturb the roots of the onions which were doing really well. Back when they were younger, she'd pull them out of the ground, knock the dirt off the roots, bite the roots off with her teeth, spit that out on the ground, and just eat the onion like that. It was a wonder she didn't die of some terrible disease, or maybe it was no wonder that she was so healthy and she hardly ever got sick.

Good and bad. A person could look at it either way.

"I wasn't expecting Tillman to be so…handsome."

"I guess I wasn't thinking that he was handsome, although he is appealing in a rugged cowboy kind of way, if you like that kind of man."

Priscilla's husband had been a white-collar guy. He had a nine-to-five job, and while his job had been in the agricultural industry, he didn't have to get his hands dirty. That had drawn Priscilla back when she was younger, and Phoebe could understand that draw. A regular schedule, someone else owning the company so all the stress was on them. The only stress on her husband would be making it to work on time, and hoping the company didn't go through layoffs, and wondering how big his Christmas bonus would be.

"Maybe I should have said he looks like a man of character. And Ezra said that he was honest and upright. I suppose that's what I meant when I said handsome." Priscilla didn't sound any less sad than she had, and her hands didn't stop moving around the onions, pulling out every single weed.

Was Priscilla interested in Tillman?

Phoebe and Priscilla had never argued over a guy. Phoebe had never been seriously interested, and their parents had been, not strict, but emphatic that dating was not a good idea. They often said that it was a much better idea to work with a person, invite them over and see how they interacted with the family, do things with them in a group, just to see what kind of character a person had. Phoebe had never gone beyond that stage, and Priscilla had ignored any red flags she'd seen in her ex.

But now, maybe Priscilla was interested in getting married again or at least pursuing a romantic relationship.

For some reason, the thought bothered Phoebe. No man had ever gotten between them, and if she had anything to say about it, none ever would. So she would clear the air immediately.

"Are you interested in him?"

Priscilla stopped, her eyes flying to Phoebe's. "No! You know what I'm going through. I don't ever want to have anything to do with the male gender again in my life! Way, way too much hurt and pain and agony. The very least is not seeing my children."

Interesting that she and Tillman had very similar experiences in their marriages. Her ex had also gotten custody of her children, and while Phoebe didn't think Priscilla was exactly bitter, she could see parallels in the way she and Tillman both acted.

Maybe they would be good for each other.

"You know Ezra has him here for you." Priscilla's voice had modulated, and she was again pulling weeds with precision.

"No. He has him here for the rodeo. And yeah, I'm working with him, but it's not for me in any way."

"Come on. Ezra wanted you and Tillman to get together back when he was in college, but Tillman married that woman who divorced him, and I bet that if Ezra were the kind of guy to say 'I told you so,' he'd be 'I told you so'-ing all over the place with that."

"I don't recall any of that. I don't even know if Ezra ever mentioned Tillman to me in any kind of way other than talking about his roommate."

"I know. His roommate. He talked about him. To you. And he even invited him to our house over Christmas break, but Tillman was already with the girl that he would eventually marry, and he didn't come."

"But that wasn't for me."

"Ezra really wanted it to be. But I often wondered if Ezra wanted the two of you to get together because he liked you and he liked Tillman, or whether he wanted the two of you to get together because he thought you were actually compatible. Ezra isn't exactly a romantic."

"No. I know."

She had never considered that. Hadn't had a clue, but then again, that was kind of the way she was. She didn't really pick up on those things. She was more practical, saw the things that needed to be done, and did them. And didn't try to read between the lines.

"Then our parents had the accident…" Priscilla's voice trailed off; she didn't really need to say any more. They all were familiar with how everyone's life had been uprooted and totally changed because of losing their parents.

Phoebe had tried to make it so that the younger children did not have the upheaval in their lives that the rest of the kids had, and she thought she had been fairly successful with that. But for all of the older kids, it had been a time of traumatic transition.

God had worked things out though. She still missed her parents, still longed for her mother, longed to just be able to talk to her, even once. There were so many things that she wanted to tell her, talk to her about, to get her opinion on, but beyond that, she had become a better person because of the loss.

"I find that really hard to believe. Ezra never said anything to me about it at all. And I think you are just making assumptions."

"You're right. I am making assumptions. But if Ezra really did play matchmaker, I think he might have been onto something. Just seeing the two of you talk and move together, you just seem…in tune with him. If that makes sense."

"I just met him. How could I be in tune with someone that I barely know?"

"Sometimes we just know. Sometimes God has the perfect person for us, and they're perfect for us for reasons that we can't even put our finger on."

"I don't feel that way," Phoebe said, but then she felt she needed to be honest. This was her twin after all. "I mean, there is some kind of…odd feeling I get around him, but I wouldn't say I feel like he's the perfect man for me, and I definitely wouldn't say that I want to be together with him or anything. He's… He's in your situation. From what I understand, it's even worse because he lost his ranch too."

"I know. I guess I shouldn't have said anything. I certainly am not interested in being matched up with anyone, and I can't imagine that he would be either, but you've been a huge help to me. When I started to get bitter, you showed me exactly what I was doing, without making me feel bad, just making me feel like I needed to do right. Maybe God has you on a collision course with him just because you'll be able to help him. I don't know, maybe it's not a romantic thing. I just can't think of anyone else in the world who would be better for a person like that than you."

Her hands paused for just a moment as she kept her eyes cast on the ground, as though there were some big secret amongst the onions. "I'd really like to see you with someone like that. Someone with character and integrity, someone who works hard and is a really great guy. You deserve someone like that."

"I deserve hell. The same as everyone else. Anything else that God gives me beyond that is a blessing that I don't deserve."

"You know what I mean. There are some people who end up married to a great guy, who really don't deserve him. You and Tillman would be perfect for each other."

"I appreciate your vote of confidence, but I'm gonna keep it in perspective, considering that you're my twin and my best friend in the entire world. I would expect you to have nice things to say about me."

Phoebe tried to lighten the air between them. She hated that Priscilla was suffering, hated that she had so much sorrow and pain in her life, and honestly she wasn't sure she wanted happiness for herself when her twin was so unhappy. Which was not a healthy attitude either, but it was the way she felt.

"Are you still thinking about moving back to Wyoming?" She held her breath after she asked that question, afraid her twin was going to say she was. She didn't want to lose her, didn't want her to move away, but it had been agony for the last year that she hadn't been able to see her children at all, and the only way to fix the situation was to move back where they could have a split time of custody.

The judge had been unwilling to demand her children be moved away for any length of time, and her husband had fought her every step of the way, able to afford high-dollar lawyers because of his family's money, not his own.

"Yeah. I want to cry every time I think about it," Priscilla said, and Phoebe could hear the tears in her voice, could almost see her eyes filling, even though they were glued to the ground where her hands still moved to pull weeds. "But every time I think about my kids getting back from school and me not being there to greet them, then spending time with the woman that my ex is living with now, and them being a family with someone else. It just…rips me up to the point where I can barely think about it. In fact, I try not to think about it."

"It's probably best to not think about the things we can't do anything about. Right now, you can't fix any of that, so I agree that it's for the best for you not to think about it."

"But I want to solve it. It's like a problem I can't let go of. How can I figure it out so that I get my kids? You know?"

"Right. And moving back to Wyoming is the best solution. It just means that you leave all of us and you're back there by yourself. We built such a network of support for each other that community is almost irrelevant. Being back there by yourself will probably be difficult, but we still have friends back there, and if that's what you need to do, then that's what you need to do."

"I was thinking about asking you to go with me, but after watching you and Tillman, I want you to stay."

Phoebe didn't know what to say. She hadn't considered moving back to Wyoming with her twin. But she was her best friend and her family. And she really didn't have anything holding her here now. Not anymore. Not with Lois graduating and going to college. Lois was the youngest and the last one that Phoebe had homeschooled. Technically the ranch could live without her, especially since Lucas had married Ryland, and Ryland was more than capable of doing everything that Phoebe did. She'd probably do it better.

"I never thought about that. Let me think about it. If that would make it easier for you, if that would make it better."

"The judge might be more inclined to give me even more time if I had someone at home who could watch my kids if I worked. If we had a two-income home. Even though we're sisters, of course."

"Yeah. Wow. I... I feel like I could really help you."

"But I don't want to pull you away from here, if this is where you really want to be, and I definitely don't want to pull you away from Tillman, if God brought Tillman here for you."

"God has sure been taking His good old time in bringing anyone here for me. I'm almost at the point where I can't have children, and while I know that's not the only reason to get married, having a family would be a big reason for me."

"Yeah. Same."

They continued to pull weeds in silence, with Phoebe rolling around the new ideas in her head. She had never considered them before, and she wished she had. She would have convinced Priscilla to move back as soon as her ex got full custody and convinced the judge that the children shouldn't travel to North Dakota on a regular basis.

It was a long drive, and it would be hard on the kids, but to see their mom?

Of course, going to pick the kids up and bring them back, then traveling that distance home would be hard on Priscilla as well. Maybe that ruling was for the best, and Priscilla moving to Wyoming would be for the best as well. But Phoebe moving with her?

Lord, please let me know what I need to do. I want to do what You want me to do, even if it's not what I want.

Chapter 8

Phoebe concentrated on hitting the stake in front of her with a hammer, pounding it into the ground, and not looking at the man who was plowing the ground in front of her.

Tillman and she had marked out an area for the arena, and now they were preparing the ground for it. Tillman had said that it could take several weeks for the ground to get worked up, dried out, worked up some more, and turned into the perfect base for the rodeo activities. It was also something they could get started on without too much money invested.

They had gone around and marked out the area, and he had gotten started tearing up the ground while she put the actual stakes in to show the boundaries.

They had worked together closely over the last two days, and Phoebe had to admit she enjoyed every second. Tillman wasn't necessarily fun to work with, exactly, but she knew she could count on him. He would do what he needed to do, and he wouldn't stop until the job was done, even if that meant he helped her with her work.

Not that she sat around waiting for someone to help her. She just appreciated someone who jumped in and did whatever was necessary and didn't draw lines, refusing to cross into territory that they didn't consider theirs.

He hadn't worried about his hours, and her initial assessment had been correct. He was going to work long and hard and not watch the clock.

Of course, sometimes folks went into a job doing a little more than what they expected to do once they settled in, but Tillman didn't seem like that was the case.

She finished pounding the stake she was working on in, then picked up the pile, carrying it to the next X they had marked out on the ground with bright orange spray paint.

He handled the tractor like he'd been born on it, and it was hard for her not to want to just stand and watch him.

But if she didn't watch what she was doing, she would miss the stake. She'd already done that one time, slamming the hammer into the muscle just above her knee. A little lower, and it would have really hurt. She needed to pay attention.

She had no sooner thought that than her eyes strayed once more to the man on the tractor.

Shaking her head at herself, she forced her gaze back to the stake, but she lost her balance and took a big step to catch herself.

She thought she'd be okay and lifted the hammer over her head to bring it down with a hard thump on the stake, taking some of her frustration out through the manual labor, but as she brought the hammer forward, the claw part grabbed the back of her head, and searing pain shot around her skull and down her arms.

She almost dropped the hammer, but years of working with her brothers, knowing she couldn't show weakness or they'd tease her, kept her hands firmly gripped around the handle, although the whack that it made on the stake barely moved it at all. She'd lost her ability to put any force behind it as her body focused on dealing with the pain.

It felt like she ripped her whole skull open, but she doubted that it had done more than scratch the back of her head. Putting her hand on the place it throbbed, she couldn't feel anything other than the sharp pain fading into a much more manageable, dull thump.

It served her right for not being able to pay attention to the job that she was supposed to be doing and wanting to make googly eyes at some guy. She was way too old for that. In fact, she didn't recall ever going through a stage like that.

Taking a deep breath, she tried to shake it off, gripping the hammer, not lifting it nearly so high, and bringing it down with all the force she could muster, which honestly wasn't much. Her strength would come back, once the pain faded away, but in the meantime, she didn't want to draw attention to herself by not working. Especially over something so silly.

Taking a deep breath, she looked off to her left, away from the buildings, at the never-ending North Dakota sky. She had been born and raised in Wyoming, and she loved that state, but there was just something wild and wonderful about North Dakota that seeped into her bones, gave her soul strength, and revived her spirit.

One more breath, and then she turned back to the stake.

As she did so, she realized the tractor had stopped and…Tillman was getting out.

Not only was he getting out, his eyes were on her as he hurried over, walking with long strides across the broken-up soil.

"You're bleeding," he said without preamble as he got close enough for her to hear him.

"I am?" she asked, looking at her hands and legs, unable to believe that she missed something else. Had she accidentally stumbled into a stake without realizing it?

"The back of your head," he said, pointing and then reaching around her to grab her shoulder and turn her around.

He didn't jerk her around. In fact, if she had to say, his touch was actually rather gentle. She appreciated that. Even as she realized that maybe it did feel like something was running down her neck. She had just assumed it was sweat and didn't think anything about it. But maybe she grabbed more than she thought she did with the claw end of her hammer.

"How did you rip up the back of your head?" he asked, and there was concern mixed with baffled incredulity in his tone.

"I cut it with the hammer. I didn't think I'd scratched it, let alone made it bleed."

"It's gushing. But I suppose head wounds typically do." He didn't say anything else, but she heard rustling behind her and glanced back in time to see him pulling his shirt over his head. "Hope you don't mind, but we need to get the bleeding stopped. At least enough so we can tell whether or not you need stitches."

"You're right about head wounds. They do gush blood, but I hardly think I would need stitches." She didn't mind at all, and in fact, it was nice to have someone taking care of her.

Not that she thought she ought to get used to it or anything, but since her parents had died, there hadn't been anyone to take care of her. Not that she needed anyone. She was the healthiest out of all the twelve kids, very seldom getting sick, and when she did, it was always a milder case than anyone else had.

She definitely appreciated that, since it was typically her taking care of everyone else. But just for a few moments, it was nice to have someone's soft touch on her, someone being concerned about her, someone…even if he was taking his shirt off and using that, at least someone making sure that she was okay.

Only for a few moments though. In just another minute or two, she was going to tell him that she was fine, and he could go back to the tractor, and she would walk to the house and figure things out.

"I'm going to put some pressure on this, just to make sure the bleeding stops. I… I think you probably ought to lie down. That's a lot of blood."

"I'm sure it's okay. Head wounds are like that, truly. I've seen enough of them in the boys over the years to know that you think they're going to die, and they don't even need a Band-Aid."

"In order to put a Band-Aid on this, you're going to have to shave your head."

"I guess it's not getting a Band-Aid then," she said, and her eyes popped wide open. She was not going to shave her head, she was not going to get rid of her hair, not even one strand of it. Whatever was on the back of her head, she was just going to have to deal with it.

"Thanks a lot for coming over. I hadn't realized that there was so much blood. But I can take it from here." She reached back to put her hand on his T-shirt to press it against her head.

His hand was there, and her hand pressed over top of his. He didn't move.

She turned her head, and his hand moved with her, as she looked up into his eyes. "Truly. I'm good. Thank you for your help, but there's no point in both of us stopping."

"The work can wait. I understand we're in a hurry, but we're not in so much of a hurry that we're going to let dead bodies lie by the road while we plow on."

She laughed. It was just so funny. The idea that she was going to die, not because someone else did something to her, but because she hooked her own head with a hammer.

"My siblings used to tease me that it took a special kind of talent to be as clumsy as I am. I have a tendency to agree with them."

"I have experienced twice now your proclivity toward clumsiness, as you call it, and I guess I would have to agree. If I were one of your siblings, I would enjoy making fun of you, because I've never seen anyone with this level of…clumsiness in my life."

"So did you say clumsiness, but you actually wanted to say stupidity? Because that's what it sounded like?" she said, a little bit of tease in her voice, mostly to cover the fact that she was extremely embarrassed. Obviously he never worked with anyone who was such a major danger to themselves.

"No. Never stupidity. Just in the couple of days I've worked with you, your mind runs circles around mine. I could never call you stupid."

That shut her up. He hadn't said anything like that in the times that they'd talked before. In fact, she might have thought a couple of times that he didn't really like her at all and would rather be working with one of her brothers.

The rodeo was important, integral to the plan they had to make the ranch solvent, but they couldn't afford to lose any of the boys' manpower out in the field and working with cattle and the dude ranch. There were things they did that she just couldn't do.

That's why Tillman had gotten stuck with her. Not some kind of matchmaking on the part of Ezra, as Priscilla had suggested. Phoebe had thought about that for all of about three seconds and dismissed it completely. The idea was ludicrous. Not only that Ezra would be a matchmaker, but that he would try to match her up with someone they barely knew. Although back when he was a roommate in college, it might have been a different story. She supposed it would be hard to know anyone better than you knew someone that you lived with.

"Hold still, I'm going to look and see if it's still seeping." Tillman's fingers moved under hers, and she realized that she still had her hand at the back of her head, although she wasn't exerting any pressure on his. She was just touching his fingers.

She was impossibly ridiculous, she thought as she pulled her hand away from the back of her head and stood still as he did what he said he was going to do.

"No. It's not gushing anymore, but it's still seeping enough that I can't really see how big the wound is."

"What does it look like? I mean, can you give me any idea of how big you think it is?"

"In other words, is she going to lose her hair over it?"

She laughed. "Yes. That's exactly what I'm asking. Thank you for the interpretation."

"No. I don't think you need to worry about losing your hair. But I'm guessing, this is just a guess because the only medical knowledge I have is taking care of other guys I worked with who got hurt, that if you don't go get stitches, you're probably going to have a scar. Which," he hastened to add, "will be hidden by your hair if you don't shave it."

"That's all I needed to hear. As long as no one with a razor comes anywhere near me, I'm good. Even if I bleed to death. In fact, I would prefer to bleed to death rather than lose my hair."

"I would not have pegged you as vain."

"And I don't usually think of myself as being vain either. And I don't typically make a big fuss about my hair, I just brush it and usually throw it up in a ponytail or something, but… I want to keep it. It's…a part of me."

The part of her that made her feel feminine. The Bible said a woman's hair was her crown and glory, and while maybe that made it so that it wasn't quite as vain as she felt, it was still more a matter of her identity being tied up in the one part of her that made her feel pretty and female.

"Surely there's something you have that you would not want to lose, that would make you feel like less of a man if you didn't have it," she prodded, wanting to turn the conversation away from her and onto him.

"Guess I lost that," he said softly. And then, after a few long, drawn-out moments where she thought about what an idiot she was and how she wished she wouldn't have said anything, he added softly, "I guess I didn't die."

But the idea that he felt like less of a man was still out there in the air. He didn't deny that. Didn't even try. Maybe he just didn't want to talk about it, or maybe it was true. It was hard to equate losing a person's ranch with losing their hair, but maybe it was the idea of losing something that he worked for, that made him feel masculine and gave him a purpose.

"You know what, let's go. I think I'll have it stitched."

"No." The T-shirt moved a bit and then pushed back. "It's still seeping, but I don't want you to lose your hair."

"I hardly doubt they'll shave my whole head to put a few stitches in the back of it. It'll just be losing a patch of hair, and I'm a big girl. I can handle it. And unlike other things…hair grows back."

They weren't really talking about hair, and they weren't talking about her being a big girl exactly, it was just the idea. Sometimes things got taken away from you, and they changed the way a person thought about themself. And for some reason, she wanted to prove that she could face it. Face the thing that she just said that she didn't want to face, didn't want to ever lose, would rather bleed to death than lose, because he probably felt the same way about his ranch.

Again, not really a comparable thing, but it was less about what they were talking about and more about what they meant.

"Are you gonna drive me to the ER? Or am I gonna drive myself in?"

"What are you going to do, park in front of the emergency doors and walk in to get yourself stitches?"

"Well, I've parked there before, and they don't take very kindly to it, because you're in the way of the ambulances, but when I'd rushed my siblings to the ER, I guess they give you a bit of a pass when it's a true emergency."

"Hmm. So you have some experience going to the ER."

"I have brothers. Of course I have experience."

"And yet, there is a man and woman here in the field, and it's the woman who's going to the ER. Would you like to rephrase?"

She laughed. "You are besting me at every turn today. I think maybe I just better shut up."

"Please don't. You…challenge me, make me laugh, and it's been a while since I felt like laughing. Since I've appreciated a challenge. Since I've…felt like a man."

She wished she could turn around and look at him, unsure exactly what he meant by those words, but instead he continued to talk.

"How about you stand here. I'll go get my truck and pick you up. You probably haven't lost enough blood to make you dizzy, but I prefer not to take that chance. Can you stay here like a good girl?"

"I might have been able to stay here if you had kept off that good girl thing, but once you said that, I will walk to your truck under my own power. I don't care if it's sixteen miles away."

"Do I need to take a hammer and smack you over the head with it in order to ensure that you stay here until I come get you?"

"I don't have to pay for my ER care if you do that." She meant it in a teasing way, but it was just a reminder that neither one of them had much of anything. Which…normally wouldn't be too bad, for Phoebe anyway. Her family was trying to get a business started, which was never easy and often rocky.

On the other hand, it was just another kick in the shins for Tillman, who had already admitted that losing his ranch made him feel like less of a man. Not having two nickels to rub together probably didn't help things either.

"Hold this," he said abruptly. "I'll be right back."

Chapter 9

Tillman strode away, angry with himself. Although he wasn't sure why. There was nothing that he could have done to keep Phoebe from hurting herself. Nothing he could do to fix it, other than take her to the ER, which he kind of bullied her into.

Not intentionally.

He hadn't meant to say the things he had, to even allude to the fact that losing his ranch had been a huge blow to his manly pride. He wasn't supposed to have any manly pride. He wasn't supposed to have his identity tied to a place or a tangible thing.

He knew that, and yet, he couldn't help the fact that he had, he did, and it had been shattered when he lost it all.

Maybe that was why the Lord had taken it away.

He had been too arrogant about it, too full of pride in himself. He didn't want to think that way, but he needed to own it, to examine himself and see what areas he needed to grow.

Still, he had been surprised at the strength of his reaction when he saw blood on Phoebe. First, he hadn't been sure what it was, and then it had been obvious that she didn't even know. He thought maybe she'd been shot, but of course, that wasn't reasonable.

When a person was in a panic, sometimes they weren't reasonable.

Which made no sense. Why was he panicking over someone he just met? Of course, she was the sister of one of his best friends from college, but still, the strength of his reaction had shocked him.

He probably shouldn't examine it too much.

He got in his truck, started it, and drove back to the field. Phoebe had gone back to work, the little turkey. She was pounding a stake in with one hand while holding his T-shirt to her head with her other.

He should have stopped and grabbed a T-shirt from the bunkhouse. They'd probably let him in the ER without one, but it would be better for him to be fully clothed. He'd stop on the way out.

All he'd been thinking about was getting her in, getting the bleeding stopped, and there she was working again.

He wanted to grab her by the throat. Except, he really didn't, he just wanted to grab her, pull her close, and hold her.

Which was crazy. And ridiculous, especially after the contortions his ex-wife had put him through. He shouldn't want to have anything to do with any woman ever again.

But in the last few days since he'd met Phoebe, he watched her be selfless, watched her do whatever needed to be done, watched her say yes every time one of her siblings needed her for something, watched her be accommodating to him and work more than her share. She must have spent hours making her spreadsheets, figuring out the things they needed, getting estimates, and getting everything ready so that they could have a discussion about things they had to have and the things that they could chop due to budget constraints.

That was going to be an uncomfortable and hard discussion, and maybe then he'd see that she would demand her way. But so far, nothing of the sort. She'd been the easiest person to get along with he'd ever met.

"What are you doing?" he said with more force than necessary when he got out of his truck after parking beside her.

"We're never going to get this stuff done if we have to take off in the middle of the day for me to go to the ER."

"This is the first time in four days. Once every four days won't be that bad."

"This is not funny," she said, although there was a small smile in her eyes as she lifted her head. But it was obvious to him she was frustrated with herself. She didn't like the fact that she was the one holding them up from work.

"This could happen to anyone. I've actually done that myself, although not to the point where I needed stitches."

"Or maybe you just didn't go."

"Getting cold feet?" he teased her, just because he thought she would have the reaction that he wanted, insisting that she go, and that would make him feel better.

"Never. I can do this. I am attached to my hair, but I don't have to be."

He laughed at her little bit of humor. "If you're not attached to it, you can let me give you a haircut when you get home."

"I don't think I want to make that big of a sacrifice," she said, with her eyes narrowed and shifting to him. She seemed to realize he was teasing her, pushing her, and maybe even prodding her a bit.

But again, she didn't get upset. She was probably used to being pushed and prodded and teased to within an inch of her life because of her brothers.

He supposed he was a typical man in that regard, where he couldn't help but pick and poke, mostly because he wanted to get a smile out of her, not because he wanted to hurt her or do anything to harm her. On the contrary, he wanted to push her into going to the ER, which is what he felt was best for her.

He put a hand on her arm, the one that held the hammer, and waited until she met his eyes before he moved his hand down to her hand and gently removed the hammer from it.

"Now you can get in my truck."

She laughed. "Maybe we can stop at the house and get some Tylenol. My head is starting to pound, and it feels like this is going to be a doozy."

"When you hit yourself in the head with a hammer, it has a tendency to hurt for a while and induce headaches."

"I see. I wish someone would have told me that earlier."

"And that would have stopped you?" he asked as he opened the pickup door and put his hand out in case she wanted help inside.

To his surprise, she took it. He almost thought she wouldn't, insisting that she could do it herself. But Phoebe didn't seem to be prideful. Which is why he was so surprised when she started talking about how she didn't want her hair shaved off. He wouldn't have thought that she had any feminine vanity, but he'd been wrong. Interesting.

Of course, his admission about feeling the same way about his ranch had shut her up pretty quick. And she was putting her money where her mouth was, so to speak.

"I need to run in and grab a shirt anyway. I should have done it when I was there before. So I'll grab some pain pills while I'm in."

"Thanks. Some water too?"

"Water, pain pills, T-shirt. I kind of feel like you're delaying the inevitable."

"No. I promise. Just grabbing the necessities. Although, the T-shirt is not exactly a necessity." She didn't seem to mean anything by those words, although he thought about them after he slammed the door shut and walked around the front of his truck. What was she trying to say?

But he dismissed the idea that she was saying anything more than he could live without a T-shirt. That was probably for the best. Especially if he wanted to stick to his determination to stay away from women. Funny how he determined in his heart that was what he was going to do, and then the Lord sent him Phoebe, who was…almost perfect. Even her clumsiness was endearing.

But it didn't matter, he wasn't going to be swayed from his position. Maybe... Just maybe, they could become friends, but they definitely were not going to be anything more.

He was going to take care of her, the same way he would take care of anyone around him, although he knew that that was probably not entirely true. If it had been one of Phoebe's sisters who had gotten hurt, he would definitely help them stop the bleeding, and then he would have found someone else to help them. But he hadn't even considered going after one of Phoebe's brothers. Or anyone else to take her to the ER. Nothing in his head except for him taking care of her.

"There's no ER in Sweet Water, so we'll have to go to Rockerton. It's…just a couple blocks down from the jail, where we first met."

If he wasn't mistaken, there was some humor in her tone as he got back in the truck and handed her first the pain pills and then the water which he opened for her. He put the shirt on while he was out of the truck, and she didn't say anything about it.

She murmured thank you for both the water and pills and downed them immediately.

"Mind if I get a drink? I should have grabbed two."

"No. Go right ahead. I wasn't so thirsty. I just needed to swallow the pills."

She handed him the water back. He wasn't thirsty at all, but…he met her eyes as he put the bottle to his mouth and took a long drink.

She looked away. He wasn't sure whether it was because of the pain in her head, or because she wasn't interested. He didn't know what he was doing, because he wasn't interested either. And he needed to remember that.

Chapter 10

Monday morning, Phoebe's headache was almost gone.

Tillman had not quite gloated when the doctor had said she should take it easy because she might have a concussion.

So the weekend had been spent with her laying low. She'd seen Tillman out and about. Even though she had been sure to tell him when she got out of his pickup after coming home from the ER that no one expected him to work over the weekend. Sometimes there would be work, sometimes there would be things that they would have to do, if the cows got out, if hay needed to be made before the rain, those types of things. But there was nothing pressing, other than they wanted to get the rodeo scheduled as soon as possible.

He just grinned and told her that on Monday morning when they had their meeting they should decide about a date for the rodeo, and he would try to have all the information he needed in order for them to make that decision.

He'd reminded her that he needed to leave Monday evening, and if she wasn't able to do her job because her head hurt too much, they could hold off meeting until Wednesday.

She had told him that she would be able to do her job. Headache or not.

She kind of wished she hadn't, because resting was a little bit difficult because of the stitches in the back of her head. The doctor had ended up putting about twenty in, although about halfway through, he lost count. One of her siblings would take them out for her. They'd done that plenty of times, saving the extra doctor visit.

Thankfully, they didn't shave all of her hair. If they had tried, they probably knew they were going to have the vain woman in front of them pitching a fit. Perhaps because they'd experienced that before.

Regardless, she and Tillman had exchanged grins over that. Losing her hair shouldn't have been quite so hard, although seeing the blonde strands lying on the cold hospital floor made her heart lurch. It was silly that she was so attached to something that mattered so little. Although, like she told Tillman, the Bible did call a woman's hair her crown. Just, Phoebe figured that a woman wasn't supposed to be vain about her crown, no matter how tightly it was attached to her head.

Grabbing a hot cup of coffee from the pot that was almost always hot downstairs in the kitchen, thanks to Alaska, she decided she'd drink it black this morning, figuring she needed it. She carried it out across the yard and through the horse barn where she nodded at her brothers, already at work, but didn't stop to talk.

Once she went through the other side, Tillman, as was his custom the week prior, was sitting at the table waiting on her, his phone out, a notebook in front of him, and a pencil behind his ear.

If she could see his phone, he'd either be working on his notes or looking up something that had to do with the rodeo. She'd glanced over his shoulder more than once, and he was always all business.

She'd actually gone on social media to see if she could find any accounts from him, and there was nothing.

She had a feeling he didn't have anything. Which made sense, since most of her brothers didn't, although Asher's wife, Sondra, had taken over the social media postings for the ranch. Her posts garnered a lot of interest, and perhaps someday would even bring in money.

Beyond that, none of them really had time to keep up a social media presence, even if they did have interest, which Phoebe certainly didn't. She had no desire to post her life online for everybody to see.

She could understand why people did that though, especially people who didn't live close to their family. But it wasn't for her. And apparently, it wasn't for Tillman either, although maybe he had deleted everything with his divorce. That's what Priscilla had done.

Getting divorced had a tendency to mark a person in odd ways and make them do things that, while it didn't erase the past, helped them not focus on it so much.

Maybe that was for self-preservation, she wasn't sure.

"Good morning," she said as she slid into her seat, setting her coffee on the table and adjusting her seat until she was comfortable, setting her phone and notebook down in front of her.

"Morning." Tillman studied her, his eyes narrowed just a little as though he were trying to take in every detail that he saw. "You still have a headache. You should go right back over to the house and lie down."

"I'll get right on that, as soon as you and I chat for a bit."

One side of his mouth pulled back like he wasn't very happy with her answer, and she admitted it was a little bit snide. She didn't mean it that way, she just didn't want him to think that he could tell her what to do, except she did appreciate the care and concern that went into those words. And that convicted her.

"I'm sorry. That wasn't very nice. I can't believe that you can even tell I had a headache just by looking at me."

"Your face is a little pinched. I was guessing more than anything."

Funny that he would admit it. It made her smile, but it also made her feel good that he cared enough to even check.

"Thanks for caring," she said, although she wasn't sure that he would even put the word caring onto it or want to admit that he did.

He just jerked his chin up, acknowledging her words without saying whether or not they were true. "I assume you weren't able to pull any figures together for us?"

"I did. Give me a few minutes for the pain pills to kick in, and it'll be like I never even saw a hammer last week."

He snorted a little, then lifted his coffee to his lips. "All right. I can start."

"Go right ahead."

He started talking about the things he figured out, and while he did, he turned the notebook so it faced her and showed her the list of things that he put together, dividing them into the three categories that they had talked about earlier. Stuff they couldn't live without, stuff they'd like to have but didn't have to, and then luxury items.

He explained where he'd come up with all of the things that he had, and told her that he couldn't be entirely sure of his numbers, but he estimated to the best of his ability.

"I also have a list of people I'm going to call once we're sure on a date." He flipped the page over. Every line on the page had a name on it. "It's actually three pages long. I assume that most of the people I call are not going to be able to make it, but the bigger names we can get here, the better. They'll draw in their own crowds. Some of them have quite a following, not just in real life, but a lot of them have a social media presence that reaches tens of thousands if not hundreds of thousands."

"Wow. Do you really think we're going to have that many people? Because I didn't plan for that many." She pulled her lip in and caught it with her teeth. She had just assumed that it was going to be a small-town rodeo and thought if they even had a thousand people show up, that would be a lot.

"I guess I would rather plan for as big a crowd as what we can and go from there. It'll be a waste of money if we plan for one hundred thousand and only get fifty, but I don't think it's out of line to say that we could probably have ten thousand." He paused. "I don't want to pry, but I think we ought to have a figure in mind that we hope to make, figure out what our expenses are, and see how many people we'll have to have in order to make the goal. I think that's what we should aim for."

"That sounds good to me." It sounded totally reasonable. They should have some kind of goal they were aiming to hit at any rate.

Not just being able to pull it off, or being able to pull it off well, but hoping to hit a certain number, make a certain amount of money, and have everyone who came leave smiling.

"That kind of jives with everything I've been working on." She opened her notebook and tapped the page. "I have all the food and everything written down here. I don't think that's going to interest you, although you can look at it if you want to. I was only planning on food for two thousand people though. If we have ten thousand, and that's what we're going to plan on, I'll be running out before the rodeo even gets started."

"I think you need to plan for more. We don't want to be unreasonable, but we don't want to run out of food either. That will not bode well for making people want to return. I wonder if there's something we can do with the leftovers if we end up overshooting our mark?"

"Yeah. I think a lot of it can go to the food bank in Rockerton, and we might even be able to give some of it away at churches the next day. I assume it's going to be on Friday and Saturday?"

"Yes, and I thought we should aim for six weeks." He put a hand up as she opened her mouth. "I know that's close, I know we'll have to work hard, but the quicker we can do it, the better. We'll get a turnaround on our money faster. Eight weeks would be almost comfortable, but if we shave those two weeks off, then we've only got one thirty-day billing cycle, and we'll have money coming in before the next one."

"I see your reasoning." She had been going to open her mouth to protest. Six weeks was…not much time. Not at all. But she was more concerned about him than her. She could have vendors lined up, maybe not as many as what she wanted, but some. And she could have the food prepared. She was going to have to do some finagling to figure out where to store it all, especially if they were going to be feeding ten thousand people rather than two thousand.

She had a little bit of experience in feeding crowds, but not crowds like that.

The vendors would help though. Some of them would be food vendors, although some of them would be the type of vendors a person would see at a flea market or a fair. Regular people who did crafts or some other type of thing to make money on the side. A lot of times, the work was of the highest quality, and it was always unique.

It was her favorite type of place to shop.

Not that she thought she was going to be getting much shopping done on the day of the rodeo. But it was fun to plan something that she knew that she would enjoy if she were a spectator.

"So do you think you can do everything you need to do in six weeks?" she asked, even though she knew he'd already set the date and wouldn't have done it if he wasn't sure. She just wanted to confirm.

"I think I can. In fact, I know I can. I did want to suggest something that you might not be comfortable with."

"All right. You've already made me uncomfortable today. You might as well keep on." She eased her words with a smile, which he saw as soon as his eyes shot to her face. It was obvious that he did not want to make her uncomfortable.

"I have to leave tonight to go to the arbitration hearing in the morning. I was hoping you could go with me. We can talk about all of this then, do our regular daily roundup, sleep on it, and spend the ride back talking some more. That will give us more time to work the rest of the week. We'll have a lot of things to work out, timelines, things that need to be ordered, and that type of thing. We should be able to work all of that out in the twelve hours we'll be spending in the truck."

"All right. I can go."

His brows lifted and his eyes widened, and she assumed it was because she acquiesced so easily. "Has anyone ever told you you're too easy to get along with?"

"When you have eleven siblings, somebody has to learn to give in. I don't really mind. I hardly ever have strong feelings, but when I do, I can dig in with a stubbornness that would probably surprise you."

He nodded. "I knew you were stubborn. I don't think I'd be surprised at all."

She laughed a little, just because of the way he said it. Like he knew a secret about her that no one else knew. Her siblings all knew about her stubborn streak, although she supposed that they often forgot because Tillman was right. She did have a tendency to be easy to get along with. Deliberately. She didn't want to be the person who was always demanding their way. Or who never had things go good enough for them.

She wanted to be the one who came up with solutions and figured out ways to get along, not the one who was always throwing up roadblocks to make everyone's life miserable. She'd been around people like that, and they weren't fun. It was much better to have a can-do attitude than to have a do-it-my-way attitude. At least in her opinion.

"All right, if it's okay with you, I'm going to go get started on my work for the day, and I'll expect that you and I will leave around five or six o'clock this evening and finish our discussion then."

"That sounds good," she said, draining the last of her coffee and standing up from her seat.

He picked up his cup and his notebook and phone. "I know it's a short time period, but I think we'll be surprised how well everything comes together."

"I don't think I will be. You seem pretty competent, and I know you know what you're talking about. If you and Tobias can get the building done, then I don't see any reason why everything else won't fall into place."

She knew she was just skimming the surface of the things that needed to be done. They would have to make chutes and pens and figure out a place to rent bleachers and job johnnies and tables for the vendors and perhaps even provide benches for those who needed to sit someplace that had a back they could lean on.

Plus, there were the showers to build, and the parking area to get ready, and they had to finish getting the ground ready, which they had been doing when she got hurt.

There was so much it made her tired just thinking about it, but she had never been one to shy away from a challenge. And it was a challenge, to her anyway, that he said that he thought they could do it. She would certainly work as hard as she could in order to make it happen.

Chapter 11

Tillman couldn't believe Phoebe had agreed to come with him. He had expected her to say that she had too much to do and she needed to get moving on it. After all, she had originally floated the idea of doing the rodeo in three months, sometime in July. He expected panic, arguments, even a bit of a temper tantrum, or maybe the silent treatment, or something.

But after her initial surprise, she'd been on board. Over the last four hours, as they'd driven together, she'd actually been very optimistic. She'd thrown herself into getting her things lined up as much as possible and assured him that she would be helping him as much as she could.

To which he responded that she could help him the best by staying out of the ER and, for goodness' sake, not picking up any hammers.

She had laughed, but he thought maybe his words had hurt her feelings just a little bit. Because she wanted to be involved, and she wanted to be considered as good as any other helper, any other man, maybe.

But she wasn't a man, and about an hour and a half ago, he'd realized that he hadn't considered that when he'd asked her along.

With any other man he would ride with, they would have gotten one hotel room, two beds, and split the bill, no problem.

But that wasn't really going to work for Phoebe and him.

At least he didn't think so. He was probably okay sharing a hotel room with her, but it didn't exactly make him comfortable to think about it. And he was almost certain that she would not want to.

He had finally decided to stop wasting time thinking about it, and when they got closer, he'd just ask. That seemed like a smarter thing to do, rather than sit around and wonder what in the world they were going to do and worry about it.

They still had some things they needed to talk about, but both of them were tired, and conversation had dropped off. Not to mention it was hard for Phoebe to juggle all of the notes they had written on notebooks in the dark, which had fallen not long ago.

"Do you think you have much chance of winning tomorrow?" she asked, and it was a total change of subject from everything that they had talked about. Ever talked about actually, since she had been careful not to ask any personal questions, and other than a few comments of his where he mentioned her shape and her hair, he'd been careful about it too.

He certainly hadn't meant anything by his other comments, he just didn't really think about it, the same way he'd act if she were a man. But he definitely treated Phoebe differently, and he didn't see anything wrong with that.

"I know I'm supposed to say yes. Confidence and all that. But I've lost everything. It's hard to think that tomorrow's going to be any different."

"Have you done anything differently to make it different?" she asked, and it seemed like a very reasonable question to him. Except he didn't know how to answer it.

"Like what?"

"I don't know. Fired your lawyer? Taken a different angle in your request? I… I guess when something doesn't work, you can try again, but if it doesn't work the second time, sometimes it's better to retreat and regroup, come out and hit it a different way, you know?"

"I guess I can fire my lawyer. He doesn't seem very competent and is much more interested in how much I'm paying him and when than he is in winning."

"Yeah. Definitely sounds like I would want to get someone different. Someone who actually seems like they're invested in me and believes in me."

"I guess everyone just thinks the kids belong with their mom. I mean, I think custody arrangements definitely tilt more toward the dad than they used to, but she really painted me like a monster. And there were things I couldn't argue with."

"That you're a monster?" she asked, a little bit of confusion in her voice, like she couldn't understand why he wouldn't argue with something like that.

"She said I lost my temper. That I yelled at her. That I scared her, and I never got physical, but she was afraid I would. I couldn't argue with any of that. I did yell at her."

He huffed out a breath and tightened his grip on the steering wheel. Why was he talking about this? He hadn't told anyone, other than his lawyer, and his lawyer wasn't exactly the compassionate, you can cry on my shoulder for a little while kind of person.

"Did you do the other things too?" Phoebe asked, and there was no censure in her voice. Just a calm gentleness that made him want to explain himself to her.

"She just made me so mad. She promised that she would stay with me. She pledged her life to mine. She told me she'd be happy wherever we went, whatever we did, as long as we were together, but it all turned out to be a big lie. And I know, things didn't turn out the way she wanted them to, and sometimes people change their minds, but you can't make vows and then just change your mind."

"I can't disagree with you. I mean, your actions should be based more upon what is right and wrong and less upon what you feel. But I guess that's not really something we're taught anymore."

"No. We're taught to do what feels good. And for her, it didn't feel good to stay married to me anymore. She accused me of a lot of things, most of them are true. I wasn't very patient with her at times. I worked a lot. I got upset when she spent more money than what we had, because we couldn't pay the bills we already owed, and she went and ran up more debt. I tried to talk to her about those things, but she would just cry and tell me that I didn't understand, and then run to the bedroom and slam the door in my face. I…eventually got to the point where I was so frustrated I would just yell at her, even though it didn't do any good. I am not proud of that."

"No." She sighed, taking a deep breath and blowing it out in a long, drawn-out sound that made him feel like maybe she had things that she wasn't always very proud of either.

"When my siblings were little, after my parents died, it was mostly me raising them, and sometimes I would get so frustrated. Any time I did, I always regretted it because Mom had always been so patient with me and with the other older siblings. It wasn't fair that we got Mom and they had to have me. I wasn't as good as Mom was, I wasn't as patient, I wasn't as considerate or kind, and I definitely wasn't as good of a teacher." She sighed. "I yelled at the kids a few times. Rufus especially just seemed to dance on my last nerve. He had a special talent for that. And he would do it and laugh, and it would just drive me over the edge."

"Yeah. Nicole definitely danced on my last nerve. That seemed to be her nightly ritual."

"But I eventually learned that it was up to me to control my reaction. I couldn't allow what they did to make me angry or to make me lose my temper, because that was allowing them to control me. I never did get to be as good as Mom, but I stopped yelling."

"Well, when she walked out, I didn't really have anyone to yell at anymore. Then she used it all against me in court. So yeah. I wish I would have had more self-control, but it ended up that she won anyway."

"Part of what I had to do was to let go of my anger and bitterness at the Lord for taking my parents." Her voice was soft in the darkness, with just the dash lights glowing in the interior, as mile after mile of flat pavement flew by.

It hit him where it hurt when she said anger and bitterness. He had plenty of that.

"I had to get that out of my heart before God could fill it with something else. I didn't want to. I wanted to be angry. It wasn't fair. I looked around at all of my friends who still had their parents. When their parents hadn't even decided to live for the Lord the way my parents had. You know?"

"Yeah," he said, his voice soft and barely audible. He wasn't really thinking about what she was saying as much as he was thinking about how it applied to him. He had so much anger and bitterness filling him that it would be hard for God to take what happened and work it for good because there was no room for any good. He was all filled up with the sour nastiness of what his wife had done and the anger and hurt that he had from it. How could God work with that? He had to let it go.

And he had never even thought about that before until Phoebe had just admitted that she had to do it in order to move on.

"So I had to take a hard look at myself. I had to look at my heart and face the fact that I was angry. The fact that I was bitter, and all of those feelings were directed at God. And maybe a little bit at the drunk driver who had run into them."

"Did he get jail time?"

"Some. Not because of our family. We didn't want to prosecute. All we wanted was for him to get into some kind of rehab so he would quit drinking and not hurt anyone else. It didn't seem responsible to let him back out on the road, but it also didn't seem very Christlike to throw the book at him. So we did the best we could at the time."

"That takes a big person. I would have wanted him to spend the rest of his life in jail for manslaughter, murder, because that's basically what it was."

"Except he didn't mean to. He just was a young kid who made a foolish mistake. Some foolish mistakes you recover from, and some foolish mistakes affect people you don't even know for the rest of their lives."

"Yeah." And he thought again of Nicole and what she considered her foolish mistake—marrying him. She had rectified that, but in the process, she had wrecked his life. And he had been full of anger and bitterness. Still was. Still resented the fact that she was off living the life that she wanted, while he was struggling to even be able to see his kids. Struggling to rebuild, and he would never have what he had and what she had taken from him.

The thought made his hands tight on the steering wheel and his jaw clench. He deliberately loosened it, moving it up and down before he made his hands relax as well.

Just thinking about Nicole made him mad.

"So you really think that taking a look at yourself, realizing you had the anger and bitterness, and getting rid of that changed things for you?"

"Yeah. Absolutely. It's kind of like you're a vessel, and you can only hold so much. If everything that's inside of you is anger and bitterness and hurt feelings and feeling like life isn't fair, and there's no room for the good that God wants to give you. I mean, God can always work a miracle, but He usually works within the laws of the universe. And those laws state that if something is already full, you can't pour more in."

That made a lot of sense to him, and it made him see that he had a lot of work to do.

He wasn't sure about how to go about it. Probably, what Phoebe said, taking a good hard look at himself and seeing the places where he'd harbored the anger, where he justified it, where he told himself that it was absolutely okay for him to be upset because she had been so terrible.

He wanted to think on that a little more, but they passed a sign that said they only had thirty miles to their destination.

"I didn't think about this when I asked you to come, but I assume we'll want separate hotel rooms."

"Oh. Yeah. Definitely. I'll pay for mine."

"I was the one who invited you." He really should be the one to pay, but both of them knew that he didn't have much money. Of course, they both knew she didn't either. "If it were nicer out, I'd suggest we sleep outside. That would negate the need for paying for two rooms."

"Then we'd get run off somebody's property for trespassing. It's probably better to pay to stay at a hotel. And I'm sorry, I should have thought about it and just said that to begin with. But I appreciate you thinking about it and bringing it up."

She made him feel like he was thoughtful and considerate. Two things that Nicole had always said he wasn't. But she thanked him for taking care of her when she hooked her head with a hammer, and even though they laughed about it, the gratefulness that she had shown toward him was still there.

Phoebe just always seemed to see the best in him, make him want to be better, to live up to what she thought about him. And when she found out things that weren't the most flattering, as she had tonight, she didn't seem to hold that against him or make him feel like there was something wrong with him.

He liked that about her. Actually, he liked her. A lot.

Chapter 12

It was a beautiful day, the sun was shining, and it was warm enough for Phoebe to sit by the fountain outside the courthouse, enjoying the weather, with her notebook open in front of her trying to think of anything that she might have missed.

It was too bad she didn't know anyone who would actually put on a rodeo like this. She would like to call and just chat for a while, trying to figure out if she covered all the angles.

Of course, with Tillman's experience, she felt like they were probably good, but it would make her feel better to know that she wasn't missing anything. She didn't want to get to the point where it was too late to fix it and realize that she had a gaping hole in her plans.

She glanced at her phone. 12:15.

Tillman had thought he wouldn't be much past twelve o'clock, and it had now been an hour and fifteen minutes that he'd spent inside the courthouse.

She flicked her phone off and put it away, saying another prayer, maybe her thousandth of the day, for Tillman, and that he would at least have one ruling in his favor.

She thought about what she told him in the truck. Something that she found to be true. That if she was full of anger and bitterness,

God couldn't fill her with something else. It was up to her to get rid of the anger and bitterness. It was a command, and she figured that God's command was for her own good. So that He could give her more, although it would be easier to do perhaps if He told her the why along with the basic command.

Don't be angry, because I can't bless you when you're angry.

But maybe they were just supposed to obey and realize that God would reward them when they did. Regardless, she didn't have any Bible to back that up, just her own experience and the things that she'd seen in others' lives.

Even though she felt like Tillman, if anyone, had every reason in the world to be upset and angry at his ex.

She'd just jotted down that she wanted to double-check the bulk food companies when footsteps behind her made her turn.

Tillman strode away from the courthouse steps, his stride fast and angry, his cowboy hat shoved down low over his head, his jaw set.

She didn't wait for him to get to her. She could tell from the way he was walking that things did not go well. Gathering her things up, she waited for him to reach her before she fell into step beside him, almost having to jog to keep up.

She didn't ask him how it went, didn't ask what the actual decision was, just got in the pickup when he opened her door and put her seat belt on in silence as he walked around, getting in and starting the truck without saying anything.

They'd been on the road for two hours before he spoke. She wasn't going to prompt him, wasn't going to push him, and figured that sometimes she needed time, and that seemed to be what he needed right now, as well.

Finally, he broke the silence as the white dotted lines flew by.

"I'm sorry."

She turned her head to look at him.

"You're sorry? For what?" Had something happened and she missed it?

"For not talking to you for the last two hours. I was angry."

"I could tell you were angry. It was pretty obvious. You don't need to apologize for not talking. I assumed that you just needed to work things out. I also assumed that things didn't go the way you wanted them to."

"To say the least." There was disgust in his voice.

"I'm sorry to hear that," she said, feeling truly sorry. "I prayed almost constantly for you, asking for God to give you at least one good ruling."

"Well, He didn't. He gave me the worst ruling ever."

She sighed, wondering what could be worse.

"The judge said that everything stayed the same. If I wanted to see my kids, I had to drive to them. He said he would reconsider after I'd held a job for a month, but considering that I'd lost the ranch, their home, and everything I'd ever worked for, he wasn't holding his breath."

"Wow. That was harsh. Unnecessarily so." She shuddered, unable to imagine that a judge could be that...nasty.

"He seems to be good friends with Nicole's lawyer, and I know that none of them would ever admit it, but I think the judge might have a thing for her. I could be wrong. Maybe I'm just making things up to make myself feel better."

She wanted to argue with him, wanted to say that a judge would be fair no matter what his feelings were, but she knew that wasn't the slightest bit true.

Lots of people, judges, elected officials, and anyone in between, used their position of power for their own gain, furthering the causes that they felt were important and not necessarily doing what their job description entailed or what they were compelled to do because of fairness and impartiality. They were human, after all.

Phoebe didn't want to be too hard on them, because she didn't know if she could be impartial if she were a judge. Her heart would bleed for a father who wanted his children, but she probably would be turned off by anger and bitterness. Not that she thought that that was the problem.

She did know for sure that God knew and had allowed it. But she didn't think that would be a comfort to Tillman at the current moment, and she didn't say so.

They drove for a little while, and then he looked over. "You never said you forgave me. You haven't said much at all. Did I scare you?"

"No. I have six brothers, remember? Your anger, your frustration, your pain is not going to scare me."

His lips tightened when she said pain, but he didn't argue. That was probably the thing. A lot of times, she noticed that when her brothers were hurt, especially emotionally, they lashed out in anger rather than saying "you hurt me."

They didn't cry, and they didn't want pity, they just wanted to hurt someone else the way they were hurting. Usually in a physical way.

"I forgive you, just for the record, although I didn't think that you did anything that I needed to forgive you for. So I suppose I was a little surprised that you apologized to begin with."

"I didn't treat you as well as I wanted to, and I apologized for it. It was necessary."

"If it made you feel better, I'm glad. Sometimes I get angry too, and sometimes I just need some time to process things. It sounds like you were dealt a pretty severe blow."

"I was really counting on getting the kids over the summer. Then I drove the whole way out here, and I didn't even get to see them. I have to make another trip if I want to do that."

"Oh! I never even thought about that. We could have gone to see them."

"They were in school. They won't be out until this evening, and then it would be late by the time we got back. I wasn't going to ask you to do that, especially since I know how pressed we are to get the rodeo figured out. But I probably will be taking next weekend to go and visit. Man, I miss them."

She could hear the longing in his voice when he said that, and it tore at her heart. She wanted to help him, wanted to ease his pain and frustration, wanted to reunite him with his children. It hardly seemed right that the separation was all because of Nicole, and yet he was the one who was suffering.

But a little voice reminded her that there were two sides to every story. No matter how much of a pill Nicole might be in Tillman's story, she had reasons for her behavior. They might not be the best reasons, they might be rather bad reasons, but they were still reasons that seemed good to her.

Phoebe couldn't help but think that she was using her children as weapons, though. Weapons to hurt the man beside her, and she hated that.

"I've been thinking about what you said about getting rid of my anger and bitterness in order for God to fill me with something else. I was not successful at that in the courtroom today, but I have four weeks to work on it until I go back. I just… I don't know if I can forgive her. She betrayed me in the worst way a person can possibly be betrayed. She made promises she didn't keep, she took everything that I've ever worked for in my life, and on top of that, she hasn't even said that she was sorry. She taunts me instead. You should have seen her today when the judge made his ruling. She didn't stick her tongue out at me, but she did everything else but."

"She sounds like a really unhappy woman. And I wish I could give you the magic formula for forgiving, but all I know to do is tell God you want to, and tell Him you can't do it without Him. And then just say the words, over and over, until the feelings follow."

"Is that what helped you forgive the drunk driver?"

"That, and I remembered what Jesus commanded us to do. He said bless those that hurt you, pray for those who despitefully use you and persecute you. It took words. I didn't always feel those words in my heart, I didn't always mean those words, but eventually, as I said those words, and I prayed that God would do a work in me, give me love for that person, give me compassion, allow me to release my anger and bitterness, and allow God to deal with that person."

She paused, remembering. It had not been easy, and she hadn't wanted to do it most of the time.

"Eventually the forgiveness came, and I harbor no ill will toward him. Part of that is my confidence that God, who is the righteous judge, will make sure that everything is taken care of in the proper time." She grinned a little. "Every once in a while, maybe I have a few fantasies about what God's going to do, but… I'm really just kidding. I truly don't want anything bad to happen to him. He was just a kid who made a stupid mistake. He hurt a lot of people, but I can relate to that. I've made stupid mistakes, I've done things that hurt people, I've been selfish and irresponsible, and… I appreciate it when people forgive me."

"Yeah. Maybe you could text me the reference to those verses. I think they're from the sermon on the Mount, which is in Matthew five?"

"I have some time. I can send them now," she said, grinning over at him before looking down at her phone and pulling up her Bible app.

It was a beautiful day for a ride and a great conversation. Maybe it wasn't a conversation about happy things, but it was a conversation that made her feel more connected to Tillman, like she could see into his inner workings and see the man of character that he was and the growth that he wanted to see in himself.

She admired him, admired that he could admit that he wasn't what he wanted to be and that he wanted to be better. She could also admire the fact that he could ask for advice and wasn't afraid that it would make him look weak or small.

She found the reference and sent it to him, hearing his phone ping with her message. They'd exchanged phone numbers shortly after they started working together, because there had been so much they needed to coordinate. But that was the first personal message she sent.

A Bible verse. That felt apt.

"I was planning on talking more about the rodeo and our plans for today. I'm sorry that I kind of got derailed. I should have known that if things didn't go the way I was hoping they would, it would throw me for a loop, and I would have trouble concentrating. I think I'm coming down now though. Thank you for being patient and not pushing me. Also…"

He paused and glanced over at her before looking back at the road. "I appreciate that you didn't make me feel like I was the worst person in the world, or remind me that I wasn't supposed to be angry, or anything like that. You just…made me feel like we're all striving to be better, and that you'd help me if I needed it." He blew out a breath. "It was a good feeling. I… I've liked working with you."

"I've really enjoyed working with you too. And I'm glad that the way I handle things worked for you. I think sometimes people want to have someone who talks a little more than what I do."

"You talk the perfect amount," he said, glancing over again and smiling this time.

"There he is. I think you're right. He's back."

"I hate that he even left. I don't know why it just can't be me. But I have so many emotions wrapped up in that, and I want my kids so bad. And it just seems so unfair."

"Sometimes I get really wrapped up in something, like this rodeo. I know it's not the same, it certainly isn't as important as family, but I was just worrying earlier about whether or not I'd left something out, and while I think I need to do the very best I can, I don't want to lie awake at night thinking about this. I just want to leave it in God's hands. I'll work as hard as I can, and He'll have to do the rest. That seems to be the way He wants us to do things. Pray like it all depends on Him, and work like it all depends on us."

"I've never heard it put quite that way before, but I have to say I agree. That's a great way of saying it."

"Maybe, maybe since there's nothing you can do with the situation with your wife and the court, maybe it just needs to be put in God's hands."

"That would probably help a lot. It would keep my hotheaded nature out of it."

"I've never heard anyone say that you have a hotheaded nature."

"I usually don't. But once I get angry, I get really, really angry. But you're right. There's no need for me to get angry. God can handle it. He was in charge today, and He allowed this to happen. Now I need to sit back and wonder what exactly He wants me to learn from that, and then try to learn it."

"Very good. I agree."

They didn't say anything for a while, and then he nodded at her notebook. "What do you have. Anything new?"

She pulled the notebook up and started going over the things that she had and what she'd been writing down while he was in the courthouse. Before she knew it, the miles had flown by and they were back in Sweet Water.

"I was so angry earlier, I didn't even think about food. At the very least, for coming with me, I owe you lunch. How about a meal at the diner? It's not fancy, but I've heard the food there is good."

"It is, and… I'll take you up on that."

Chapter 13

Phoebe wasn't sure going to the diner constituted a date. It was really just repayment for what she had done for Tillman. She didn't feel like he owed her, but she was starving, and supper at the ranch would be long over.

He held the door while she walked in the diner, and they chose a booth along the side.

There weren't too many customers and they were able to order their food, which was brought out in a short amount of time.

"I wondered how long it would be before the two of you were dating after I heard that you two were working together. Ezra is quite the matchmaker. Not like Sweet Water needs any more of those. We certainly have enough to go around," Maisie said as she set the food down in front of them.

Phoebe had her mouth open to refute what she had said, but she didn't get the words out before Maisie left. She turned horrified eyes to Tillman.

He looked a little shocked, a little amused, and a little annoyed.

She was not going to apologize, although the words *I'm sorry* were on her lips. She had not done anything wrong. Not a thing. He was the one who had suggested they eat at the diner, and she had actually wondered if it was a date. Not seriously, but the thought was there in her head.

"I didn't realize that was the way this was going to look," he murmured softly, a thoughtful tone in his voice.

"I guess I should have known. I've lived here longer than you."

"I grew up in a small town too. I know how it is. I just…wasn't thinking. I was appreciative of what you did and hungry. That's all that was going through my mind. I promise."

"I was hungry too. And that's exactly what I was thinking about. Although, I suppose I did think when you said it that it sounded a little bit like a date, although I laughed and dismissed that immediately. Because I knew that was not what you meant."

He picked up a French fry and dipped it in the ketchup that he squeezed down on his plate. "I determined in my heart when Nicole did what she did that I was never going to trust another woman again. I was done, completely and totally, with women."

He kept dipping his fry in the ketchup, moving it around, belying the fact that he said he was hungry, acting like he didn't care if he ever ate.

She didn't know what to say, other than that was exactly what Priscilla said, and she was in a very similar situation as to what Tillman was. Phoebe could understand why he would feel that way.

"I hadn't counted on meeting you." He looked down at his plate, then he looked back up at her. "Don't read anything more into that than what there is. You're just a nice girl. A nice woman. Nice, and that makes me feel that maybe the way I feel about women wasn't entirely fair. Then maybe, maybe if I had enough time, like you gave me those two hours of silence in the truck, but a lot more time, maybe I might not feel that way about all women forever, if that makes sense."

She thought she understood what he was saying. He wasn't interested in a relationship. And wouldn't be for a very long time, but that wasn't an insult against her.

"I think sometimes when we go through bad experiences, we feel exactly the way you do. That might be a bit of a survival mechanism. Kind of the way after a food makes you sick, you don't ever want to eat that food again."

"Women and food. Every man's downfall."

"I don't think so. Truly. I know that my opinion has to be biased, since I am a female, but I really don't think that all women are what Nicole seems to be. And maybe, maybe it's just a matter of her needing to grow up. Or something else."

She couldn't make excuses for Nicole. There were no excuses for blowing up a person's family just because she wanted something different. Especially when the person that she was married to wanted to work things out and she refused. It was hard for Phoebe to find it in her heart to excuse that in any way, but only God knew Nicole's heart.

It wasn't really up to her to judge, although she wanted to.

"Thanks for understanding," he said, and then he put the fry in his mouth.

"You know, we need to say something to Maisie when she comes back, or the entire town is going to think we're dating. I don't really care. Small towns are going to talk, but it might be good to just put the effort into trying to nip that in the bud before it gets spread all over town."

"So you don't mind being linked with me?" He grinned a little, although there was still the effect of the day in his gaze, the tiredness and the weariness, which made her think he was tired of fighting, tired of the effort, and that made her sad. "After all, I'm the new guy, and you know how small towns are about new people. Do you really want to have the reputation of taking up with someone that nobody knows anything about?"

"They are going to talk, and I don't really care what they talk about. I guess things that aren't true bother me, so I'll want to correct it for that reason, but beyond that, what people say isn't going to get me worked up. I'm more interested in what God thinks of me than what others say about me. He knows my heart."

"And it's a good heart," he said, with more confidence than maybe she thought he should have felt for all the better he knew her.

"Sweet Water's a good town. And Maisie means well. I wouldn't trade my small town for anything."

He pressed his lips together, like his experience in a small town was slightly different. "I really like the way you think the best of people. I probably should be more like that."

"Maybe you have reasons for not."

"I feel like I do, but a lot of times, we feel like we can justify our actions, but in reality, we're just taking the place of God. Instead of allowing God to work and allowing Him to make judgments, we do it ourselves."

She couldn't disagree with that as she speared a piece of broccoli and put it in her mouth, chewing thoughtfully. He had said it all. That was the bottom line. God was in charge, and everything they did should show their faith that He was a righteous judge and would work things out the way they should be worked out.

"I heard there's a rodeo going on at the Sweet View Ranch," a voice said beside their table, causing Phoebe to turn.

She recognized one of the Powers brothers. They owned Powers Trucking company and feed mill on either end of Sweet Water.

"You heard right. I sure hope you're planning on coming."

"What day is it? I just heard, and I haven't gotten any details."

"Six weeks from Friday," Tillman said while Phoebe grabbed her phone and pulled up the calendar, counting out the six weeks and giving him the date of June 10th and 11th.

"Wow. That's fast."

"We're hoping it's not too fast," Phoebe said, maybe being more honest than she needed to be.

But it made him laugh. "That's the way to do it. Make a plan and hit the ground running, doing it with all your heart. That's the best way to live life."

Phoebe's eyes met Tillman's. She couldn't know what he was thinking, but she wondered if it might be along the same lines as what she was, concerning their earlier conversation. The one where he wanted to be careful that he didn't get hurt again. It seemed to be the opposite of jumping in and living life with his whole heart.

From the look on his face, she got the feeling that might be exactly what he was thinking. She wanted to smile, but she didn't.

"Just want to let you know that Powers Trucking is behind you. My whole family has been excited about it ever since we heard it at church on Sunday. If there's anything we can do to help you out, just let me know."

"That'd be great," Phoebe said immediately. "We really appreciate your support."

"And you know, I'm not the only one with an attitude like that. There are a lot of people who would like to see this succeed. I'm sure you'll have help wherever you need it."

"I appreciate that. Thank you."

He nodded, jerked his chin at Tillman, and then he said, "I think I saw Billy around here somewhere." He winked before he walked off.

"Billy? What was that about?" Tillman asked, with a furrow in his brows, as Phoebe felt her cheeks heat even though she tried to keep them from it. If only there was a way to keep her cheeks from turning bright red every time she was embarrassed.

"Well, before my family moved in, Sweet Water used to have a steer that ran the streets."

"Like a wild steer? How did he castrate himself?"

"Yeah, that's a good question. Actually, Billy has an origin story which I've heard, but I don't know if I remember well enough to share the details. I just know he had a reputation in town for being a matchmaking steer."

"You're kidding? A matchmaking steer? I feel like I've heard everything now."

"You probably have. But there are people who actually swear by it, and there are at least ten couples who say Billy is the reason they got together. It's kind of hard to argue with people who say that they wouldn't be together except for Billy."

"I suppose one couple might be stretching the truth a little, but ten? That does seem like overwhelming evidence."

"That's how I feel about it too. But that was years ago, and the Sweet Water veterinarian, Lark, took Billy so he could retire on her farm. She and her husband, Jeb, have given him a nice home in his old age. Although, being a matchmaking steer wasn't exactly the most notorious thing Billy was known for."

"Really?"

"Yes. Some people said that he was in love with a pig. Munchy, I think her name was."

"This town just gets weirder and weirder, if that's possible."

"I think it's cuter and cuter. I mean, what's not to love? A matchmaking steer? A steer in love with a pig? And a town that loves them all. Plus, couples who got together because of Billy definitely have a fun story to tell their children and grandchildren."

"I see. And he was warning us…or maybe he was basically saying the same thing that Maisie was, only he was saying it like a man."

"That's a really good deduction. I would have to agree with you."

He grinned at her over the table. "Well, I told you, I like you. So maybe, you should be the one who's concerned with all the warnings. If you're going to run, looks to me like you better get started."

She was going to say something funny, give a smart retort, but then she remembered about Priscilla and needing to move to Wyoming, and she closed her mouth before any words tumbled out. She might end up running, although not on purpose.

"Hey. I wasn't trying to push you. We're friends. That's what I was thinking anyway. I mean…mostly."

"No. It's not that. I was going to say something about me running, just in a smart way, but then I remembered that Priscilla, my twin, might be moving to Wyoming, and maybe I really will be running away. I don't want to, but I can't say no to my twin when she needs me."

"I wouldn't want you to." He said the right words, but there was a sadness to them, almost a depression. Like he never expected to have anything more than dregs from the bottom.

She hated that he thought that way, and she hated that she might be making that thought come true in his head.

"That's not a bridge I have to cross right now. She is not going to Wyoming until after the rodeo. At the very earliest. She just… She can't stand being away from her kids. She's in a similar situation as you are."

"Then I feel bad for her."

Phoebe nodded, and they finished their meal in silence. The banter that had been between them, and even the little smile and the glimmer of hope, had been crushed. Phoebe didn't even know if it would be right for her to try to fan it into any kind of flame again, since it might just be false hope.

He paid for their meal, and they drove home in silence, both of them deep in thought. What neither one of them were probably thinking was the fact that man couldn't see what God had planned. Things would have felt a lot different if they had.

Chapter 14

A loud pop ripped through the stillness of the kitchen.

"That always scares me," Mina said with a gasp of surprise as she looked up at Phoebe opening a can of biscuits.

"I'm sorry. I should have warned you. It scares me too. Sounds like something is exploding. Which, when you think about it, something kind of is."

"Yeah. That's okay. I should have expected it. I know we need them for the Christmas morning biscuits and gravy casserole. I really appreciate you getting up early and helping me with this." Mina gave a smile that melted Phoebe's heart.

Like Phoebe was doing something special by getting up thirty minutes before she usually did.

"You know I'll do it. And I enjoy it too. I bet your class is going to be thrilled."

For her home ec class, Mina was supposed to bring in a casserole that would feed everyone. They were trying out different casseroles, since the home ec had been tapped to provide food for the school board meeting later that month. Each kid in the class was bringing in their own special recipe, then they'd vote on them all and choose one to make and serve.

This was a recipe that Mina's family had made back when Mina lived with her mom and dad.

The thought made Phoebe sad. Mina seemed like she'd mostly adjusted and that she loved living on the ranch. In fact, her mom had reached out, asking for Mina to come visit, if not come back to live, and Mina had instead asked her mom to come to the ranch and spend some time. She hadn't wanted to go home.

That thought tore at Phoebe's heart too. She'd been so blessed to have both mom and dad. Of course, they'd been taken away from her in an accident, but at least they hadn't fought, hated each other, gotten divorced, and created separate families with other people. Talk about instability in a child's life.

But people did the best they could, and sometimes things just didn't work out. Maybe they could work harder, try harder, do more, but for Phoebe, she knew there were times where she felt like she was doing everything she could and things just didn't work.

Tillman's face came into her mind at that point. He had tried as hard as he could to keep his family together. He was willing to work things out with his ex-wife. But she just hadn't been willing. And he freely admitted there were things he could have done better. Things he wished he would have done better.

People just didn't get do-overs.

Phoebe tried to shove those thoughts aside as she enjoyed working in the kitchen with Mina. Mina needed steady, stable influences in her life, and Phoebe intended to be one, for whatever time Mina was with them. She wasn't going to question God's timing or His plan. She would just do the best she could with whatever got put in front of her. Right now, that was Mina.

"That sausage smells so good," Phoebe said as Mina stood next to the stove.

"It's always so hard not to eat a little bit before we put it in."

"It would be even harder if my brothers were in here. Sausage and bacon are like impossible to resist for them."

"I've noticed." Mina laughed a little, and then she sobered, looking around the kitchen. "Aunt Phoebe, can I ask you a question?"

Phoebe resisted the urge to point out the fact that she just had. "Of course. What's wrong?" She could tell by Mina's voice that there was something bothering her.

"You and your sisters and your brothers, you've kind of become my parents. It's weird, but I just look at all of you as people who are raising me."

"I'm glad. I look at you as a child who is my child. In fact, I was just thinking as long as God gives you to me, I am going to do my very best to be the best example I can to you."

"You guys always say that I'm supposed to do my best, like you just said. Because of God. He wants us to do our best."

"That's absolutely true."

"Sometimes at school, kids tease me for trying to do my best. If I get an A on a test, people make fun of me. It's like… It's like you can't be smart and cool at the same time."

Phoebe didn't know what to say. She really didn't have any experience in this. Her mom had homeschooled her, and she had homeschooled her younger siblings.

Since Mina was an only child, and since no one at the ranch technically had custody of her, they thought it was best to send her to school. Just to head off any issues that her parents might eventually have. Since they could fight over anything, they didn't want to put red flags up by homeschooling her, since while it had lost a lot of its stigma, it still sometimes made people think that a person was far out and totally weird…and that was Mina's problem.

"You know, I wish I had wise words for you. But we aren't homeschooling you because we're afraid of what people are going to say. Especially if either one of your parents ever think there's a problem here. We wouldn't want them to come down on the schooling methods, that's just one more thing for them to pick on."

"I would love to be homeschooled!"

Phoebe almost asked if she thought she'd be lonely at the ranch, but she closed her mouth. There was always something going on at the ranch, and when she was being homeschooled, they had access to so many activities, they often had to pick and choose which ones they really wanted, because they were too busy to do them all.

"Maybe that's something I can talk to some of the others about, especially Claudia, since she makes a lot of the decisions regarding your care." Claudia was friends with Mina's mom and had been the one she had asked to watch her child. Claudia brought Mina to the ranch, and everyone had just kind of pitched in.

"I already asked. She said she'd pray about it. But I guess what I was thinking was until I find out for sure whether you guys will homeschool me, I don't know what to do at school."

"To begin with, we can get the names of the people who tease you, and we can take them to the principal's office. But I think sometimes in life, people just aren't nice. And we have to learn to let the things that they say to us roll off us. Now, in life, you can usually get away from people. You don't have to sit right beside them in class, or eat lunch with them, or anything like that. If you really hate your job, you can try to find a different one. You can eat outside in your car, for example. But if you're working with someone you truly don't like, a lot of times, you need to figure out a way to learn to either like them or to get them to like you."

Phoebe knew that what she was saying to Mina probably wasn't what the school counselor would say. But it was like the verse that she had just given Tillman not that long ago. The verse that said to pray for those who despitefully use you and persecute you.

"I have a Bible verse I'd like to send to you. Is that okay?" Phoebe asked, pulling up the reference and copying some verses.

"Sure. Is it going to help?"

"Maybe. I think it shows you that even two thousand years ago when Jesus walked the earth, there were still people who made fun of other people, and He had some commands for us to use. Not that they're easy, and not that that's going to just make the whole situation go away. I don't want you to think for one second that it's going to."

"Someone told me that most of the time, you have to walk through hard times, they don't just disappear. I think that was one of your brothers talking about my family and how my parents are fighting and how I wish that I could just have a family again, although… I really like it here. The more I'm here, the less I want to go back."

"I'm really happy to hear that," Phoebe said as Mina walked over and put her arms around her waist. Phoebe squeezed tightly. She wished she could protect her from all the harmful things that happened in the world. She wished she could keep the bullies away from her, keep the kids who wanted to tease her for doing well away, keep her protected from all of the bad things.

But that wasn't the way life was supposed to be. There were going to be bullies. There were going to be hard things. There were going to be things that Phoebe didn't think a child should have to go through, and rather than avoiding those things or trying to get them taken away, it was better to help Mina learn how to handle those things. To let her know that there were no easy outs in life. And if there were, it often was to a person's detriment to take them.

"Now we just have to make sure we take it out when it's done," Phoebe said as they slid the casserole into the oven.

"I have enough time to go get ready," Mina said as she closed the oven door and set the timer.

"I suppose I should comb my hair and put some clothes on that I'm not afraid of being seen in in public," Phoebe said with a smile, looking at her jammies and imagining that her hair looked wildly crazy.

"It smells good in here," Tillman said as he walked in the back door.

Phoebe had forgotten about her hair until she had just said something, and then Tillman walked in and made her want to put both hands over her head or at the very least grab her hair and put it up in an impromptu ponytail.

"I'm making Christmas morning sausage and gravy casserole for my home ec class today. I'm in a competition with the rest of the kids in my class to see who has the best meal to serve the school board at their meeting later this month."

"I think I could be a very good judge of that."

"Then you'll have to come to my class every morning."

"Don't tempt me. There's not a whole lot I won't do for some good food. And that smells really, really good." Tillman grinned at Mina, and then his phone rang from his pocket, and he pulled it out.

"Excuse me," he said, looking at Mina first and then Phoebe. "My kids are calling."

"You can stay in here. Mina and I were just leaving, and it looks like it's raining outside," Phoebe said as she walked toward the door. She knew he typically spoke with his children in the evening after he was done working. And sometimes she'd seen him on the phone over the weekends as well. He never said who he was talking to, but when it was around lunchtime or in the evening, she assumed it was probably his children.

When they had their morning meetings, which they'd been doing for the three weeks he worked there, he had never been on the phone with them.

But it made sense that he would talk to them before they left for school.

Since they'd come back from the mediation date, they hadn't talked much more about his children or his ex or about any of the personal things that were going on in his life.

Phoebe hadn't said anything more about Priscilla and Wyoming either. Priscilla wasn't leaving until after the rodeo, maybe to make a decision easier for Phoebe.

Regardless, their conversations had been mostly business, although since the trip, there had been a friendlier overtone to their interactions.

Still, they'd set a very difficult task in front of themselves, and it was going to take all of their concentration and efforts to make it happen. They didn't really have time to be distracted by the personal things that were going on in each of their lives.

But she didn't think he was against being a little more personal. She made a note to ask him if everything was okay when they met later that morning. Humming to herself, she followed Mina up the stairs to get ready for her day.

Chapter 15

"We're up, Daddy. You told me to call you." Erin's voice sounded high and cheerful in his ear. But Tillman detected a note of sadness as well.

A nine-year-old shouldn't have to get herself and her brother out of bed in the morning. They should have a parent there doing that for them. But this was modern day, and he supposed there were a lot of children who were expected to have responsibility like that, except that was probably because their mother worked, not because she was still in bed with a hangover.

"That's a good girl. You guys are up in plenty of time. Rowan's up, right?" He'd been so excited to have a son. He loved his daughter, wholly and completely, but he assumed that she wouldn't share his interests, not that Rowan necessarily would, but he had been excited to have a little boy that would be interested in driving tractors and raising cattle and learning to ride broncs and rope and do all the things that Tillman loved.

Of course, if Rowan had different interests, Tillman wasn't going to be upset about it, but he had felt his family was complete when their son had joined their daughter.

Little did he know how things were going to turn out.

"He's up. He's still sucking his thumb, though. I told him he had to stop. Mom's boyfriend told him he was going to dip it in gasoline and set it on fire to make him stop, so he hasn't been sucking it in front of him."

"I don't think he's actually going to do that," Tillman said, trying to tamp down the anger that wanted to rise up in his chest at the idea of another man thinking it was a good idea to dip his son's thumb in gasoline.

He was even angrier that Nicole would be with someone like that.

Of course, it didn't sound like she was overly happy, since her drinking had seemed to spiral out of control. He wished the children had told him what was going on before the court date, but maybe it hadn't been noticeably bad at that time.

"Are you guys gonna be able to get something to eat? Is there cereal and milk in the kitchen?"

"I don't think so, but I made microwave oatmeal yesterday, and it didn't turn out too bad. I think I put too much water in it, so I'm going to put less in today."

"Can you read the measurements on the back?"

"I wasn't sure what it was."

"If you can take me there and put me on FaceTime, maybe I can read it for you."

He waited while she went to the kitchen and got her phone on FaceTime. It was funny that she was able to do that with her phone, but she couldn't figure out the measurements for oatmeal. Modern children.

Regardless, he had been in touch with his attorney, telling him the things that were going on at the house and hoping that would sway the judge's opinion toward him.

He really didn't want his children in a house like that at all.

At times, he'd been tempted to call child services, but he wasn't sure he wanted that kind of complication in his life either.

Plus, he had been thinking about what Phoebe had said about emptying himself of all bitterness and hatred, and he didn't want to do something against his ex out of either of those two emotions. He knew he still harbored them both, but he was working on it and praying about it. And trying to have faith that God was going to do what he didn't think was humanly possible to do, and that was forgive his ex and let go of the bitterness he had toward her.

"I think I hear Mommy," Erin said after he helped her find the correct measuring cup in the drawer.

"All right. You be sure to call me if you need me. I can answer any time."

He needed to talk to Phoebe about what was going on at the house. He just…didn't want her to think he was worse than what she already did. She'd mostly seen the worst he had to offer, other than him losing his temper, which he hadn't done since the divorce.

Still, he hated the fact that he looked weak, because he didn't have his family in order, had so many personal problems. He wanted to at least be able to do his job with competence.

But with these issues and him fielding calls from his children more and more often, he was going to have to say something. If this was going to be a problem for her, maybe he should just forget about the dreams he had for his life, and the things he wanted to do, and get a job as a cashier at Walmart or something. It might not be what he wanted to do, but it would be something he could do that would be closer to his children.

"You guys have a good day. I love you."

"I love you, Daddy," Erin said, and he could just picture her passing the phone to Rowan's ear as Rowan said, "I love you, Daddy. Come get me."

They hung up before Tillman could say anything else. The words pierced his heart. Oh, how he wanted to go get his son and his daughter and bring them back with him.

He didn't know a human being could feel this longing and pain and still function.

He stared at his phone for a few seconds before he allowed his hand to drop to his side and took in a deep breath. He had to get his head in the game, the work game. He had to put the thoughts of his children and what they were going through aside. He couldn't do anything about it right now, and his time was better spent trying to do a good job and make this rodeo a success for the ranch where he hoped to work for the rest of his life. He didn't like moving around, didn't like going from job to job, he liked to put down roots, settle down deep, and establish routines that would last a lifetime.

He knew that was kind of old-fashioned too, but that was just the way he was. An old-fashioned kind of guy.

"Is everything okay?" Phoebe said, coming into the kitchen looking a little different than she had, her jammy pants gone, the jeans and sweatshirt that she usually wore as her work outfit firmly in place. Her hair was in a ponytail, and her face was freshly scrubbed but devoid of any kind of makeup.

She looked fresh and young and beautiful to him, and despite all the turmoil in his chest, the longing for his kids, the frustration that things weren't working out the way they were supposed to, the annoyance that he couldn't provide for them the way he wanted to, and the devastation that his wife had caused when she'd torn apart his family, all those things were there, but on top of it all was a joyous peace that had been dominating his feelings more and more.

It seemed like the more time he spent around Phoebe, the more he felt that joy and peace that combined into a happy feeling, a feeling like everything was going to work out okay.

"Yeah. I need to talk to you. But it's raining this morning. Where did you want to have our morning meeting?" He didn't want to talk in the kitchen where anyone could come in and hear. This wasn't something that he wanted the whole world to know. Not that there was anything he was doing that was wrong or illegal, he just…wanted it to be private.

"I was going to take Mina and drop her off at school today since it's raining, and she has the casserole to take. How about you ride along, and on the way back, we'll chat? If we need more time, we can just sit in my car until we're done."

"That's great," he said, knowing that it would be a little bit hard for him to take Mina to school, because it would remind him of his own children and what he wasn't doing with them.

But at the same time, Mina was a sweetheart, and he loved that Phoebe and her family were taking care of her when her homelife was so bad. If anything ever happened to him that he couldn't take care of his children, he would appreciate people like the Clybornes stepping in and helping him out. Trying to make sure that his children had the best childhood possible.

"I think the casserole is supposed to come out in about five minutes, and we'll leave as soon as we can after that."

Mina came into the kitchen then, bringing her sunshine smile and eagerness to share her recipe with the class.

They were in the car shortly after and had an enjoyable ride to the school. Phoebe and Mina were obviously comfortable with each other, and Tillman listened as they chattered about the different things that were going to be happening at the school soon. They also said something about an orchestra in Sweet Water and the performance that was coming up.

Tillman had heard a little bit about it, and he thought one of Phoebe's sisters was actually in charge of it, but he hadn't heard enough to be sure. Maybe Claudia.

"All right, kiddo. I love you. Have a great day," Phoebe said as Mina got out. "And be careful with that. It's still really hot."

"I will. I love you too. See you tonight."

Phoebe had a little smile on her face as Mina walked off.

"She seems like a great kid. Despite all the stuff that's going on at home. I always thought kids who were going through stuff like that would be sullen and withdrawn and angry at the world."

"Mina's special. But I also think her mom sent her to us because she was hoping that Mina would have a good influence, something steady and something that she can lean on if she needed to."

Phoebe looked over at him as she pulled out of the school. "I know you're worried about your kids, and I think children are a lot more resilient than we give them credit for. In fact, Mina and I were just talking this morning about an issue that she's having at school, and I was thinking about how we can't make our kids' lives perfect, you know? That we can only try to show them how to go through their trials so that they become stronger and wiser. It's not smart for parents to try to make every part of their children's lives perfect. We… We make it so that they're unable to handle things when they actually do show up in their lives, because they haven't built that strength up yet."

"I guess I needed that pep talk today. That's kind of what I wanted to talk to you about. It… It actually does have to do with our business meeting."

"All right," she said, looking over at him again, concern and compassion in her eyes.

He wanted to ignore that. Wanted to steel his heart against it, but he also agreed with her, when she said that maybe not all women were like his ex.

Maybe there was a part of him that thought that he just attracted that kind of woman. Or that he was attracted to that kind of woman for some weird, twisted reason. But maybe, maybe he just made a bad mistake, a stupid decision, and God was actually going to give him another chance, a chance to have a life with the woman who was…pretty much the opposite of his ex.

Chapter 16

"In the three weeks since we went to the arbitration, my kids have been calling me more often. I think my ex is spiraling down, and maybe the relationship she has with her new boyfriend isn't going so well."

Phoebe glanced at Tillman again across the seat as she drove away from the school.

She knew what he just said was not good, but she couldn't really chalk the feeling that she had up to that. There was a fear that had taken hold of the bottom of her backbone, seeming to squeeze tight, that he would be going back to his ex, that they would reconcile and patch everything up.

She wanted that. Truly, if that was God's will and if that was best for them, but in a personal, selfish way, she didn't want that to happen at all. She had gotten used to the idea of having Tillman around, not just used to it, she looked forward to working with him, enjoyed his presence, and…wondered sometimes if there might be more between them.

She'd thought that time of her life had passed her by, but being with Tillman, she almost felt like maybe she could fall in love. Maybe God really did have someone for her. Maybe there really was someone she just felt comfortable and completely at ease with, someone she worked well with together, and someone who could handle her crazy family. Someone who loved the things she did and wanted the same things she did as well.

It was a little early to see if Tillman was all that, but she definitely had a feeling of rightness when she was with him.

"Are they okay?" she asked, trying to focus on the children first. What she wanted really didn't matter if it wasn't best for them. And the best thing for them would be for Tillman and his wife to get back together.

Right?

"I think so. Erin started calling me in the morning whenever she gets up so I can make sure that she's up for school. That was after there was a day two weeks ago and two days last week where their mom didn't get up and they missed the bus, before I had Erin start calling me. So far, that's worked."

"Wow. That's terrible. Maybe the school will do something."

"Nicole had the kids lie. She sent an excuse in saying that Erin had a stomachache and then it went away. And then she said that they had no hot water, I think. Anyway, she's making up excuses so it doesn't look like it's her bad parenting. And she's told Erin and Rowan not to tell anyone."

"They told you."

"Yeah. And… I told my lawyer, although I don't know if it's going to do any good. It doesn't seem like the judge has much compassion toward me or much concern about the kids having contact with their father."

"Surely the judge typically makes good decisions. And I've been praying that the Lord will work this out so that you get to see your children. I have confidence that He will."

"I'm glad you have confidence, because I found that I really don't. I just want them so much it hurts." He lifted his shoulder up and looked out the window before he spoke again. "Anyway. I've been on my phone more than I usually have, and you've been really great with my hours and not micromanaging the stuff that I do. Most of my phone calls are about work, calling buddies of mine to pull in favors to get them to come to the rodeo and to get them to spread the word to their friends. I think we're going to have a pretty big turnout, although I haven't wanted to say anything until I get complete confirmation."

"That's exciting. And whatever you have to do with your children, I've already told you, that's more important than your job. It'll still be here for you whenever you're back. But your kids come first."

"I really appreciate you saying that. Although, I wasn't sure if you meant it. Sometimes people just say things."

"I know. And I don't want to be one of those people. Maybe you'll have to remind me about it. I haven't noticed that you slacked off in any of your work, but I have noticed that you work on weekends, and you show up earlier in the morning then you need to and stay later at night."

"I love what I do. It's hard for me to knock off in the evening, and I want to jump out of bed and get started in the morning."

"And no one asked you to do that. You do it on your own, and I love it and appreciate it. So whatever you need to do with your kids, it's okay. You've already put in way more time than anyone expects."

"Thank you. I really do appreciate it."

She could tell he was sincere. She could also tell that the conversation wasn't easy for him. He didn't want to be patted on the back for his work ethic. It was just who he was. And he didn't want to have to deal with his kids because his wife wasn't able to or because she was hungover, or whatever was going on.

None of that was anything that he wanted to handle, but he was manning up and doing what needed to be done.

Phoebe thought again of Mina and how she had told her that sometimes you just have to do what needs to be done, whether you want to or not.

Phoebe didn't like to say that and tried to give her some specific strategies, but life wasn't easy.

Of course, there were things that children shouldn't have to endure, like mothers who were hungover and didn't get out of bed. Like parents who fought and argued and didn't stay together. Like bullies at school. Unfortunately, they lived in a fallen world, and all of those things happened.

Phoebe thought a little bit about trying to be a light in a dark world. Trying to be joy and happiness in a world that was full of pain and suffering. Trying to reflect Jesus to people who didn't know Him.

It was hard to do that when a person's own life felt like it was lying at one's feet in ashes.

Joy in the midst of suffering. Peace in the midst of the storm. Love in the midst of hate.

That didn't mean that sin wasn't sin and shouldn't be dealt with. After all, Jesus showed love and compassion, but He also told the woman at the well to go and sin no more. He didn't hang out with her in her sin. He called it out.

It was hard to do that in love.

"You're deep in contemplation this morning. I thought we were going to be having a work meeting."

"I guess God's trying to speak to me about something, and I'm not sure what it is. You're going through a hard time, Mina is going through a hard time, your kids are going through a hard time, Priscilla is going through a hard time… There are so many people around me who are going through hard times, and it seems like the lessons for me are for people in hard times, but that's not me. I'm content with my life. Yeah, my heart hurts for you, it hurts for Mina and Priscilla and your kids, and for Ezra and the finances of the ranch, but I just have a peace. I'm not worried. I'm not concerned. And…if truth be told, I'm a little hopeful."

"Hopeful?"

"Maybe about the rodeo. Maybe about some other things," she said, not wanting to tell him that she was a little bit hopeful about the relationship that was developing between her and him. That's exactly what she was hopeful about. But maybe it was a premature hope, and she didn't want to get the cart ahead of the horse.

"I wish I had that optimism."

"I think it's from the Lord. I honestly do. I… I used to pray that God would give me love and compassion and grace and peace where I felt anger and bitterness and hatred and sadness after my parents' accident. Of course, He didn't do that right away, but as I look back over the years, I can see that gradually taking over my soul, and as I emptied myself of the anger and bitterness, God filled it with the things that I wanted."

"I suppose that's inspiring and encouraging, but I have a long way to go."

She didn't say anything, because she really didn't think there was much to say, and after another mile or two, he said, "I've been wanting to tell you about the people that I have who have committed to coming to the rodeo, but I didn't want to get your hopes up until I was sure."

"Are these the people that you've been spending so much time on the phone with?" she asked, remembering that he said that not all the time that he spent on the phone was with his kids.

"Yeah. I've been calling pretty much everyone I know and asking them to call everyone they know. I said that I'd really like to make this the biggest privately held rodeo of the year. I think I might even be able to have the PRC—which is the professional rider circuit—sanction it as an actual event. If that happens, we're in good. Ten thousand might be on the low end."

"You're kidding!"

"Dead serious. I didn't want to get your hopes up, but I'm feeling very optimistic. The PRC isn't in yet, but I had a verbal commitment from my contact there. The only thing that's left to do is for the committee to vote on it, and he said it's almost guaranteed."

"That's amazing. Such great news." She could hardly contain her excitement. She wanted to tell her siblings, the whole world, she wanted to stop the car and get out and talk to the Lord, thank Him for His amazing provision, but she tried to contain her excitement and focus on all the things they needed to do so she didn't drop the ball on her end.

"I think we'll definitely need to have a little bit of time in the parking lot once we get to the farm, because I need to get my notebook out and make sure I have everything covered. All of a sudden, I'm nervous."

"Don't be nervous, just be happy."

His eyes glowed as she met them with her own, and something happy and bright and excited seemed to pass between them, but it was also laced with…something else. Something that she would almost term attraction. She wished that they were sitting at the table behind the horse barn, because it felt like the kind of thing where he would take her hand in his, and they would lean forward and…

She shook her head. She was definitely allowing her daydreams to get ahead of her.

Clearing her throat, she said, "All right. How about you go ahead and start with all the things that you're planning on doing today, and the things that we still need to do, and any ideas you have for me. Once we get home, I'll get my notebook out and we'll go over that too."

She could tell it was going to be an awesome day.

Chapter 17

Mina bit a lip in concentration as she used an elbow to hold the heavy front door of the school open, carefully carrying the hot casserole, oven mitts underneath it, as she struggled to get into the school.

She went through the metal detectors balancing the casserole and trying to make sure her book bag didn't slip off her shoulder.

This was her absolute favorite food ever. Maybe partly because it brought back memories of her family being together, but also because it just tasted so amazingly delicious. How could they not vote this to be the very best food to serve for the school board meeting?

There was no award, no compensation, she wouldn't even get a ribbon. It was just the idea that her recipe won.

It would make getting up early and doing the extra work worth it. Although, spending time with Aunt Phoebe was fun, and she'd get up and do that even if there wasn't competition involved.

"Hey there, teacher's pet," a sneering voice said, but Mina did not turn.

Phoebe was right. She knew that she just needed to do the right thing, and she couldn't expect bad things not to happen to her. It was just… She hated being teased and made fun of, especially in front of other people. It made her feel…like she wasn't as good as everyone else.

She already felt a little bit like that since pretty much everyone else in the school had lived there all their lives, and she was new, even though she'd been there for more than a year.

Small towns were like that. People were new forever.

Even if she lived here for the rest of her life, people would still tell her she was new.

"What? You ignoring me now?" The voice came closer, and Mina tried to take a calming breath, but her steps quickened. She wasn't far from the home ec room, just around the corner and down at the far end of the last hall, and that hall wasn't nearly as crowded as this one.

"Goody-goody, what's the matter? You think you can get away with ignoring me?" Now he stepped into her line of vision, a kid who wasn't that much taller than she was and who she might have thought was handsome if he hadn't been making fun of her. He wore a black shirt and black pants that hung low on his hips. Way low.

"Somebody make sure you record this, we'll put it on social media," the kid said as he started to lunge forward.

Mina jerked away, but in doing so, she lost her grip on the casserole, and it started to slide out of her hands.

"Hey, Mina," a different voice said, this one with a low tone of…almost camaraderie in it, like they were good friends, only she didn't recognize that voice. And she was busy trying to catch her balance, although the arm around her shoulder and the body next to hers made it a lot easier. A hand reached out and grabbed the hot casserole.

"Ouch," the voice said, but it was a low murmur, not a yelp, and the big hand did not let go.

It had to be burning his fingers, but if it was, she couldn't tell, and neither could anyone else.

"I didn't know that was your girl, Nash," the kid in the black T-shirt said.

"Well, now you do," Nash said easily, although his eyes were hard when Mina glanced over at him. They narrowed a bit, drilling down into the black T-shirt kid. "I'd hate to hear that you were doing anything except being absolutely courteous to her. Opening doors, giving her your seat, making sure that bullies don't mess with her. Right, Dylan?" Nash said in that same, low tone. Almost lazy in its slow drawl.

Nash. Nash Olson. He was…one of the most popular kids in school. A three-sport letter winner and also known as one of the smartest kids in his class.

What was he doing with her?

Mina didn't say anything, and she kept walking, tucked in beside Nash Olson, his big arm around her, everyone else giving them a wide berth, including the black-shirted bully.

"Sorry, Nash, I didn't know. You're right, from now on, I'll make sure she gets everything she needs and that no one else lays a hand on her, that everybody treats her with respect. She's your girl, that's what she gets."

"Thanks. I knew I could depend on you."

Nash's eyes flickered a little before they turned the corner, going down the less crowded hallway.

No one followed them, although Mina could practically feel eyes boring into her back.

She waited until they got at least twenty feet down the hall before she whispered in a voice she could hardly hear herself, "What's going on?"

Nash laughed a little. "I just thought you needed a little help. I've been watching for a couple of days now, and I didn't want to make a big deal, didn't want to get into a fight—my parents would be pretty jacked at me over that—but… I didn't want to see you suffer anymore."

"Wow. I wasn't expecting anyone to step in and save me. I just talked with my aunt this morning, and she told me I was going to have to do this on my own."

"On your own with Jesus maybe?"

"Yeah. Yeah, I mean, of course she said that, but Jesus doesn't always show up in person."

"No. Sometimes he sends other people to do things that you ask Him to do. And… I don't know, this morning I just felt a huge push to go over and put my arm around you. It worked. I honestly hadn't been sure whether or not it would."

"Well, thank you for listening to the prodding."

"Thank you for praying that I would be prodded. I'm feeling like I've done my good deed for the day."

"In my eyes, you definitely have," Mina said, a little disappointed to know that it wasn't some secret crush Nash had had on her that caused him to come over and put his arm around her, but it made it that much more sweet to know that he was willing to be a hero and risk being ostracized just to save her.

Of course, knowing that he would have done it for anyone made it far less special. And despite herself, she found herself being disappointed. She did want Nash to save anyone, of course, she wanted him to be that kind of person, but she wanted to be special too. To him.

"I might have to get a statement so I can give it to my parents. They don't always think I'm very hero-ish."

"They just push you so that you fulfill your potential. It's great that you have good parents." She'd seen them in church. Both of his parents were active participants. They were there every Sunday. Nash had several older brothers and sisters who had graduated and moved away, according to the girls in her Sunday school class.

He was two years older than she was, though, so they didn't really hang out much, even in youth group. They both had their different friends they typically hung with.

"If you say so. Sometimes it seems like they push just to make my life miserable." He laughed a little. "I'm kidding. I know they don't. And I wouldn't have accomplished what I have, not that it's that much, if my parents hadn't been pushing me and making sure that

I do what I know I'm supposed to. So I do appreciate them. Even though it might sound like I didn't just then."

"Not really. You just sounded like a teenager."

A special teenager. One who would take the time to rescue a girl being bullied in the hall.

Then she remembered about his hand. She had the oven mitts back underneath the casserole, and somehow he had taken it from her without her even noticing, but she said, "What about your hand? You grabbed the casserole dish, and I heard you say ouch, and I know it's really hot. Are you okay?"

"I think so. I'll run some cold water over it in the bathroom after I get you to…home ec, is that right?"

"Yeah. Are you sure that's all it's going to take?"

"Yeah. It's not like it just came out of the oven or anything. You must have been in the car for twenty minutes or so. It was just hotter than I expected, and hotter than I would have chosen to touch if I had a choice."

He was tough and strong, and that made her heart twitter. She tried to get it to stop, but it just wouldn't. So she ignored it and focused on keeping her stride steady, pretending that it wasn't a big deal to have Nash Olson beside her.

And for the record, his arm was still around her.

She wanted to fan her face. No, she wanted to run to her girlfriends and tell them all about it. Except, she didn't want to leave Nash's side.

"So, since I saved you from the bullies, and you called me a hero, would it be too much for me to ask if we could be friends?"

Her eyes opened wide, and then they fluttered like the wings of a butterfly stuck in a net. She tried to get a hold of herself and make sure that her voice didn't come out in a shrill squeak.

"Yeah. I want to be your friend. I… I don't think I'll ever need to save you from a pack of bullies in the hall, and I doubt I'll ever be able to help you with your homework, but maybe you'll find something good for me to do."

There, that sounded reasonable, plus, the words came out and she didn't really think about them. But they were true. He didn't need her, not like she needed him. Not needed exactly, but their friend relationship definitely didn't feel very equal to her.

"Maybe I just think you're fun and funny. I've been watching you in Sunday school and in youth group, and you always look cheerful. Even though I know that your life hasn't exactly been a bowl of cherries."

"You can say that again." He noticed that she always tried to put on a happy face? "Thanks for noticing. I… I guess I just decided I'd rather be happy than miserable."

"I think it takes some people a really long time to learn that, so I'm impressed that someone as young as you are didn't just learn it but put it into practice."

His compliment made her feel good from her head the whole way to her toes, and her heart seemed to expand and fill her chest.

They'd made it to the home ec door, which meant that he took his arm from around her shoulders and opened the door, pulling it open and allowing her to go in first.

She loved the manners that he showed, the courtesy, and just the fact that he'd seen that she needed something, and he wasn't afraid to put himself out there, potentially risking his own reputation in order to save hers.

"Looks like you're early," he said.

"Yeah, I was excused from helping with serving breakfast to the elementary school today, which is what my class usually does, since I was bringing in the casserole."

"I see. I… I realize that we have another problem."

"Oh?" she asked, her hands out to take the casserole from him. But he made no move to hand it over.

"Yeah. There's the small problem of everyone who was in the hall now thinks that you're my girl, Dylan's words, not mine," Nash said with a curved-up grin that made Mina's heart flip over twice.

"Oh. Yeah. Sorry about that."

"Not your fault. It was what I had intended, but I hadn't gone any further in my planning than thinking that if they thought you were with me, they wouldn't pick on you anymore. I hadn't considered what might happen…after that."

"Oh," she said, realizing what he was saying. Now the whole school thought that they were together.

"Well…" She swallowed, unsure of what to say. How could she make the suggestion that they ought to just stay together because she liked him anyway? Except, that wasn't fair to him. "You suggested that we be friends. Maybe… Maybe we can just be friends."

"Friends who eat lunch together?" he asked, in an even softer voice.

"Okay. Yeah, I'm okay with being friends who eat lunch together."

"Maybe friends who walk out of school together after last bell?"

"Yeah. Those kinds of friends too."

He nodded. Then he said, "Maybe friends who walk into school together too. Just in case the bullies are there tomorrow."

"I can meet you in the parking lot. I usually ride the bus, but I can walk around."

"All right. What's your bus number? I'll get there early and watch for you at the end of the sidewalk."

She gave him her bus number, and he lifted his brows. "I don't want to push you into anything you don't want."

"You're not. I guess I just hadn't thought about later. I hadn't even thought about now. I appreciate what you've done, and I guess…I'm happy to be…friends."

"Friends."

He lifted his brows. She nodded, and then it felt kind of awkward when they just stared at each other, and she had this crazy urge to walk forward, but she didn't.

She remembered so many of her Clyborne adopted family saying that their parents had told them that dating was a bad idea. That it was a good idea to just hang out with someone, in a group if possible. Working with them would be even better, since they'd get to see their character and how they handle things that don't go their way. Even though Mina thought Nash was quickly growing into a man of character, she supposed that the friends thing was the best idea.

Even if she was a little disappointed.

Chapter 18

"And I think that's all we have to do, like that's not enough," Phoebe said as she tapped her notebook.

"We can do it. We still have three weeks, and things are coming together better than I ever thought."

"I feel the same way, except…I'm scared too. We can't really afford to have anything get in our way."

"If it does, we'll just work through it. But for now, I think it's time to get to work." Tillman started to stand, but he paused and sniffed the air. "Do you smell smoke?"

Phoebe's eyes widened. She hadn't been thinking about it, but now that he mentioned it…

"Yes!" She stood quickly to her feet, trying to think of where the smoke could be coming from. "We had some guests here this week, but we only do campfires in the evening. We shouldn't be smelling the campfire from last night. But I can't think of any other reason why anyone would be burning anything," she said as she sniffed the air again. Definitely it was clogged with smoke. She could actually see that the horizon was slightly blurred out because of the big cloud of smoke, which she hadn't noticed until just then.

How could she have been so involved in everything that she hadn't noticed smoke?

The horse barn wasn't on fire. She could tell that from standing there. The back door was open, and they could see the whole way through. Everything seemed fine, even if the horses did seem a little restless from what she could see of them in their stalls.

"It's probably nothing," Tillman said, but his actions belied his words as he left his notebook on the table, along with his phone, and moved around the building so he could get a better look at the house.

"The house is fine," he said, although Phoebe had caught up to him and walked by his side and saw that the house was not on fire at the same time he said it. She had remembered to turn the oven off, she was sure of it.

But there was definitely smoke in the air.

"The hay barn is on fire!" her brother Asher hollered as he went jogging by. "We've already got the fire company on the way. We're grabbing hoses from every spigot we can possibly find and pouring water on the fire."

He disappeared around the edge of the barn.

"I'm going to follow him. See if I can help."

"I'll be right there. I'm going to grab our books and put them somewhere safe." She didn't want to lose all the work that they'd done, and those notebooks contained most of it. Although they did have notes on their phone, the notebooks held far more information.

It wasn't that she didn't feel a sense of urgency to help with the barn, but she knew it was full of hay. If it was on fire, it was almost certainly going to burn to the ground. And that was not her being doom and gloom, it was just her experience. A barn full of hay was almost impossible to put out. She'd never seen it done before or heard of it, either.

Not that she wouldn't work as hard as she could to put the fire out along with her siblings. It was just…probably not going to happen.

She grabbed the notebooks from the table, tucked them under her arm, and jogged through the horse barn, and the previously quiet morning had seemed to explode in activity, with her siblings running everywhere, and she noticed several people who must have been guests on the ranch. She hadn't had much contact with the guests lately, since she was no longer doing much cooking and her entire being was pretty much focused on the rodeo.

Regardless, she raised a hand at the newcomer, who called a greeting to her, but she didn't stop. At the house, she burst in the back door, throwing the notebooks on the table and seeing Alaska turn from where she was staring out the window.

"Ezra texted me that there was a fire," she said. "What's going on?"

"I heard the hay barn's on fire. You should be safe here. It's plenty far away, and even though the implement shed might potentially catch fire, or even the small animal barn, you'll be fine. You and the kids will be absolutely safe in the house. The first priority will be to save it."

"I wish I could help. But I wouldn't be much help with two small children."

"No, but maybe you could direct the firemen to the proper place, in case they don't see it when they pull in."

Phoebe wasn't sure whether that was a good thing to do or not. It would probably be obvious to anyone who arrived where the fire was. Already she could see flames leaping to the sky from the hay barn as she hurried back out of the house and met Priscilla coming toward her with a bucket.

"Here, we're going to use the spigot in the yard. We don't have any more hoses, but we can fill up buckets."

"Is this going to do any good?" Phoebe couldn't help but ask. It seemed like an exercise in futility.

"It's probably not, but I can't just stand there and watch it burn, you know? Maybe once the firemen get here, I'll be able to just step back and give up."

"Yeah. Okay, I get that," she said, taking the bucket that Priscilla handed her and hurrying to the spigot that came off the well that had been dug in the yard of the big house.

"We should order more hoses," Priscilla said, "in case this happens again."

"I don't think if we had a hundred hoses we would be able to put the fire out. Once hay starts to burn, it's like a tinderbox."

"Yeah. I guess. I just…want to find a solution."

Phoebe understood what she was saying, but she also understood the futility of throwing a bucket of water on a raging fire. It just wasn't going to do any good at all. Even the firemen probably weren't going to do much besides keep the fire from spreading anywhere else.

When the fire trucks pulled in, Phoebe was filling up her fourth bucket.

She watched Alaska run out with the children, directing the fire trucks to the fire that was already at least three stories high, the flames leaping in huge grasping waves, black and orange and angry colors mixing with the cheerful blue of the North Dakota sky. Funny how a day that was so happy and wonderful could have turned so dark and sad. Aside from the thousands of dollars' worth of hay that had been in the barn, the structure itself was going to be a huge loss. But it would have been a lot worse if it had been the house.

That in itself made Phoebe grateful, and she said a silent prayer of thanks. Laughing a little at herself that she was thanking the Lord, when the firemen hadn't even put the fire out yet. But how could she not thank God for sparing the house? And she assumed there were no fatalities, since no one was ever in that barn except when they were going in to get hay.

Which made her wonder how in the world it had caught on fire. Maybe the faulty wiring.

"I guess that's it," Priscilla said as she stopped beside Phoebe, her bucket empty, her hair bedraggled, her face dirty.

"I guess. I'm just wondering how in the world that barn caught on fire. No one's ever in it unless we're getting hay."

"I heard that one of the kids from the people who are staying at the dude ranch was smoking behind the hay barn with his girlfriend.

That's something I overheard one of the guests talking about, so I don't know for sure if that's it or not."

"Oh, that makes sense. They probably flicked their cigarette over their shoulder and never gave it another thought."

"Exactly. We should maybe add a little bit of fire safety to some of the things we talk about when guests first arrive. Most of them probably don't understand how combustible a barn full of hay is."

"Yeah."

She watched the barn, the oldest structure on the property, continue to burn as the firemen stretched out hoses and other paraphernalia from their trucks and ran toward it. Ezra, his face black with soot, spoke with one of the firemen.

Phoebe imagined that they were probably checking to make sure that there were no people trapped inside. Or animals, although she doubted the firemen would risk their lives to save the lives of the animals.

At least she hoped they wouldn't. As much as she loved her animals, she wouldn't want a person to risk their life for them.

A tall figure with the firemen, although not dressed in fire gear, caught her eye.

The fire company in Sweet Water was all volunteer, and it wasn't uncommon for men to leave their job and go directly to a fire, especially if they thought they could help out in the early stages.

But…that figure was Tillman.

She smiled as he held onto the hose and helped the firemen drag it to the closest position they could get to the fire.

He seemed to know what he was doing as he worked with the other men. Perhaps he had been a volunteer firefighter in his hometown before he moved.

Regardless, Phoebe found her eyes drawn to him, caught on him, and not wanting to look at anything else.

"I do believe he's a good man," Priscilla said from beside her. She'd totally forgotten that her twin was standing there.

"I think so too. It's been…fun working with him. I'm kind of surprised to say fun, but it has been."

"It's always fun to work with someone who does their share or does more than their share. And does it well. Work stops being a chore and starts being something you look forward to." Priscilla obviously knew what she was talking about, and Phoebe had to agree. "I can see you two together. Have you given it any thought?"

"He's too wrapped up in the drama of his ex and whether his children are being taken care of, and he just has a whole lot of things on his plate. The last thing that man needs is to step into a relationship, especially a serious one, which is the only kind of relationship I would be interested in."

"Yeah, we weren't exactly brought up to be one-time flings, were we?" Priscilla said with a humorous laugh.

"No. Definitely not, and I think that's right."

"Sometimes, no matter how hard you try to do the right thing, no matter how well you think you know someone, they can change. Or hide their true selves."

"I know. I feel so terrible that things didn't work out for you. I wish there was something I could do. I was just as buffaloed by your ex as you were. I believed him when he said all the things he did to you. I thought you guys would be together forever. It stinks."

"Yeah. It does. But if you're going to take a chance on a guy, Tillman's a good bet."

"I'm thinking in the same direction, but I'm also thinking the things that I just told you. He's not ready."

"I wouldn't let him slip away." Priscilla gave her a last smile and then said, "I think I'm going to go into the house to make sure Alaska and the kids are okay, and get cleaned up a little. There's going to be a lot of work to do once the fire is out. Although, most of it's going to need to be done with big equipment."

"Yeah." Phoebe didn't say anything more, but she just wondered how much that was going to cost. They had insurance, but she had no idea whether that would be covered under it or not, and in her experience anyway, insurance companies had a way of wiggling out of covering things. They almost always paid a claim less than what it deserved, but she supposed they followed the fine print, which was necessary.

She didn't know how long she stood there watching Tillman work, even going so far as to move a little when he went around the side of the building, holding the hose so it could spray at a different angle.

She thought about Priscilla and the mistakes she had made, although they had seemed like good decisions at the time. A person never got any guarantees. That was pretty much the only guarantee life would give you. There were no guarantees.

She was standing beside the driveway when a car pulled in.

Recognizing Mrs. Greene from church, she smiled as the lady got out of her car and hurried over, carrying a container in her hand.

"I'm so sorry. My husband is on the fire company, so I knew he was going out to a fire at your place. I was in the process of getting supper ready, since I have a meeting this afternoon, and I thought I would go ahead and bring you guys the salad. I'm sure people are going to be hungry, and whether it's your family or whether it's folks who come to help, I wanted you to have some food to feed them."

She handed the container over.

"Why, thank you. That's awfully kind of you. I suppose I should be in the house working on cooking up a meal. Because you're right, people are going to be hungry."

"Oh, that's what neighbors are for. You're probably in shock, although it could be worse. It could have been the house."

"I said a prayer of thanks for that very thing not that long ago," she said. "I'll make sure you get your dish back."

"I have my name taped on the side. No rush."

Mrs. Greene hurried back to her car, and Phoebe stood holding the dish. It looked like the firefighters had pretty much given up trying to put out the fire, and they were just making sure to dowse the area that was closest to the next building, the small livestock barn.

She hadn't moved to go in the house when she noticed Tillman walking over. His face was covered in dirt, and his hands were filthy as well. He had rolled up his sleeves, and his muscular forearms were covered in soot and ash and dirt streaked with water from the hose.

"I've been keeping an eye out for you. I started to get worried when I didn't see you."

"Don't worry. I think I have a little bit more intelligence than to run into a burning building."

"As I've been fighting this, I've been thinking about how this is going to set us back for the rodeo."

"I wondered that too, but I really don't know. The insurance should cover the rebuilding, even if it doesn't cover the debris removal. I think it will replace the hay as well, although I don't know what it was valued at. The price of hay has gone way up since we purchased it."

"Yeah. That seems to be the way it goes. You never quite get what you need to out of it."

"Sounds like you've some experience," she said, hoping that her comment invited him to say more if he wanted to. Although, they should be talking about the rodeo instead. But really, they couldn't know how this was going to affect them until they knew what it was going to cost.

"Just a few auto claims. It's never quite what you need and never quite fast enough, and there's always a loophole where they get out of paying for something that sets you back. You sit there and scratch your head and wonder why you had insurance in the first place."

"Yeah. That sounds very familiar."

She smiled, because what else was there to do? They could get upset about it. Fine print was fine print, and when a person bought insurance, at least for her, she never really thought about all the things that could go wrong, or in case sometimes she did, it was just too expensive to add all the contingencies onto it. They couldn't afford to pay the deductible if they were covered for every single little thing.

The insurance company couldn't afford to stay in business if they covered every single little thing.

"I'm sorry about this," Tillman said after a few moments of just standing and watching the flames burn.

"Not your fault. And there's no reason to be sorry. It's a blow, for sure, but it's not a shock to the Lord."

"No. I suppose it's not." He kept his eyes on the flames and said, "It's kinda fascinating to watch fire burn, in an odd sort of way. I've always been drawn to flames."

"It must be a human thing, because I've been standing here holding this salad, knowing I should go in the house and help start cooking, and all I can do is just watch the fire. It's fascinating in a grotesque sort of way."

"I'm already on the payroll, but you know if there's anything I can do, I'll help out. And I suppose if this means that we need to shut down the rodeo, or postpone it, or something…"

"Again, I think it's too early to know about that, but I'm sure there'll be a family meeting later. And I'm sure you'll also be invited. I heard Ezra say that he said that you could come the next time we talk about farm finances. You're here, you're working just as hard as any of us, you deserve to know."

"Thanks. I guess I would like to know. It's always good to know what you're working toward."

"Yeah. You inspired me when you said that about the rodeo. I thought maybe we were being a little too ambitious, but when you're working toward something, and you know exactly what it is, it makes it a little bit more tangible. You know?"

"Yeah."

They stood for a bit more, and Phoebe got the feeling he was just enjoying standing beside her. Like she grounded him or something. She definitely felt more at ease when he was beside her.

"All right. I suppose I'd better head back. I just… I wanted to make sure you were okay."

The look he gave her made her stomach do a slow turn and made it impossible for her to move her eyes away from his.

It was almost like he was saying he cared, in a special way, about her.

Of course he cared. He cared about everybody on the ranch. They all did. But he hadn't gone out of his way to make sure that anyone else was standing away from the fire, just her. That made her…special.

She swallowed against the sudden tightness in her throat. "Be careful."

She figured he would be. He had children to live for after all, but she wanted him to know that she cared as well.

"I will be," he said, his face turning up into a small smile.

Their eyes held for just another second before he turned and walked away. She watched his easy stride, the way his arms swung at his sides, the confident manner in which he held himself, his wide shoulders and firm direction.

Priscilla was right. He was a man worth taking a chance on. If only he didn't have so many things happening in the background. She didn't want to wait forever, although…she figured she probably would.

Chapter 19

Tillman looked at the still smoldering pile of rubble in the early dawn light.

It wasn't time for him to meet for his daily morning meeting with Phoebe, but he'd been too restless to stay in bed. Once his eyes were open, he'd had to get up and do something, even if it was grab coffee and walk out to see the ruins of what had been a barn two mornings ago this time.

He was surprised that there were already people standing around and more cars coming down the driveway. A big diesel motor rumbled, and he looked over to see a tractor trailer hooked to a lowboy hauling a D9. Guys were already unstrapping it, and smoke puffed out of the D9's stack.

Several dump trucks must have come in during the night. They sat lined up as though waiting to get filled with debris so they could haul it away.

Last night when he talked with Ezra, he had said that there were people in town volunteering to come out and help in the morning, but Tillman hadn't realized how big that was going to look. Tractor trailers weren't cheap, that was quite a donation. And a D9? Even as he thought that, headlights hit him as another tractor trailer turned, hauling another lowboy, this one with a track hoe on it.

He'd worked heavy equipment some when he was younger, and moving it from place to place was expensive. Operating it was expensive as well. And yet…Ezra had said volunteers were donating resources.

This must be the donations of resources, which was a lot more than Tillman had thought. He had imagined maybe someone was going to come with a hammer and help build a fence to keep guests away from the smoldering ruins or something.

He hadn't actually thought people were going to donate their livelihoods, in such a huge way, coming to help clear things off so a new barn could be built.

Several ladies got out of the car that just pulled in, reaching into the back of their vehicle, grabbing casseroles, and carrying them to what Tillman could now see were tables that were set up in the yard of the big house.

A hand clamped down on his shoulder. "I had some phone calls after you and I talked last night," Ezra said as he strode up beside him, coffee mug in hand, a pencil behind his ear, and his shirtsleeves already rolled up, despite the morning chill.

"I see. I wasn't expecting all of this when I woke up this morning."

"No. I guess I wasn't really expecting it either, but Sweet Water is that kind of town. We have ladies bringing breakfast, lunch, and supper, and by breakfast, lunch, and supper, I mean there are at least six or seven ladies providing each, so it should be quite a spread. I wouldn't miss it if I were you. It'll be better than a church social."

"I'm hungry. Bring it on."

Ezra laughed. "I was just coming over to see if you have your CDL or can operate heavy equipment. Coleman's sent a couple of their trucks over and a few older buckets, but they couldn't spare enough drivers today." Ezra grinned. "Or maybe you have that little black book of yours that seems to be pulling this rodeo together out of thin air, and maybe you can get us some drivers out of that."

Tillman figured Ezra was mostly joking, but he happened to be asking the right man the right questions.

"Got a buddy I can call, and I operated heavy equipment shortly out of high school for about five years until I saved enough to put a down payment on a little bit of land. I've got my CDL too, so put me where you need me. I'm here to help."

"Those are magic words. Actually, magic has nothing to do with it. I just had a sense of peace when we were fighting the fire. I knew we were going to lose the barn and all the hay in it. I don't think we're going to replace that, since it was valued for about a quarter of what it was worth with the insurance company after hay prices went up last year. But I just figured God was going to work things out."

"He has a way of doing that. I don't know why it surprises me every time, because it shouldn't."

"Same. Throughout my life, He's worked in so many different ways, I should just look for it, instead of wondering what in the world we're going to do."

Phoebe had mentioned a few times about the different ways God had provided for the farm, and Tillman figured that was what Ezra was talking about.

"Just let me know what you want me to do. I'm here to work," Tillman said again, and Ezra nodded his head.

Then he grinned. "I'll make sure you get food. The truck drivers often are the last to eat, since they're not around when the food gets spread out, but I'll make sure you get a nice plateful. Actually, I'll put Phoebe on it. She can be quite a dragon when she wants to be."

"Really? I haven't seen that side of her."

"Not a fire-breathing dragon, loud and obnoxious, but the kind of dragon that…doesn't let anything stand in her way when she has her eyes on the goal. Kind of like this rodeo. I figured putting you and her together would make sure it actually happened."

Interesting.

"So we're both dragon people." He sighed. "If that's how you talk about your friends, I can't imagine what you say about your enemies."

"I say that about people I like." Ezra winked as he walked away, and Tillman grinned.

Phoebe wasn't a dragon. She was sweet and soft-spoken, but he supposed Ezra was right, she was a determined woman and worked as hard and long as anyone. If that made her a dragon, working toward a goal, putting her whole heart and soul into it, then yeah, Phoebe was a dragon lady. He could get used to that idea, and he definitely liked it.

He found himself working the bulldozer to begin with, which was slightly bigger and newer than the one he had used when he was a teenager, unsurprisingly. It wasn't hard to figure out. Bulldozers weren't exactly complicated pieces of equipment, although this one was more electronic than what he had been expecting.

Regardless, he was able to move some of the debris so the track hoe could scoop it up. After a few hours of that, he ended up in a truck hauling the debris.

He couldn't believe the people who had shown up to help, and it made him grateful to be part of such a welcoming community. People didn't just peek out of their curtains to see what was going on, but they actually went over and offered to lend a hand. A great hand, it turned out, since as he was going back for his second load, he got out of his truck in time to see Phoebe walking over, her hands underneath a big plate of food.

"So, there was a lot to choose from, but I tried to remember all the things that you seemed to like over the last five weeks, and I grabbed what I thought you would enjoy. It's a good thing too, because you see the Swedish meatballs? They're gone."

"Swedish meatballs? Man, it's been years since I've had those. I hope they taste as good as what I remember from my childhood."

"Oh, it's Mrs. Humphrie's recipe, and it is amazing. They're always the first thing to go at the church suppers. You can thank me later."

"Looks like they're loading me up right away. Want to come along with me this time?"

He wasn't sure where those words came from. He hadn't been expecting to ask her, maybe just wanted to say thank you for the food, which he truly did appreciate, since his stomach had been growling for the last hour and half.

"Well… I hate to leave when everybody else's working, but there really isn't any need for me. Lunch is over, and the ladies who are bringing supper haven't shown up yet."

"We'll be back before that. Unless we get caught up somewhere. It only takes four hours round trip."

"All right. Let me text Priscilla and let her know. It looks like they have you almost loaded now."

"It doesn't take much to get the weight on with this kind of thing." It made him a little bit sad to think that they were hauling her barn away, but she seemed okay with it. It was a very practical way to look at things. After all, there wasn't anything they could do about it except go on. If someone had died in the fire, he was sure things would be a lot different.

"Did they figure out how it started?" he asked, knowing that he hadn't been around to hear any of the news that might have spread while the men were standing around waiting to be useful.

"One of the kids who were at the dude ranch was smoking a cigarette behind the barn. I heard that yesterday, but it was confirmed last night by the fire marshal. I guess he was with a girl, but it doesn't really matter. She wasn't smoking and didn't touch the cigarette. It was all him."

"Now what?" he asked, digging into the food that she had brought, closing his eyes as the meatball hit his tongue and reminded him of the joys of childhood.

Some of them anyway. His childhood hadn't been great, but Swedish meatballs were a bright spot.

"I'm not sure. I… I guess our farm insurance covers the dude ranch aspects, but I'm not sure what the fine print says about fires our guests start. I guess we'll find out."

"On the bright side, you don't have to worry about paying for any of this."

"Exactly. We don't. Everything here is donated, and even the demolition place where you're dumping is giving us a discount on taking the debris in. I mean, obviously they still have to pay to take it somewhere themselves, so they can't really do it for free, but it's just overwhelming sometimes how generous and considerate and compassionate people can be. It makes me want to be a better person, you know?"

That was exactly right. That was what he had been thinking all day. As people pitched in, it wasn't even his farm, but he saw them giving sacrificially. It wasn't nothing to donate a truck, let alone heavy equipment. And yet people did it anyway.

If push came to shove, Tillman had wondered exactly what kind of person he would turn out to be. The kind who took or the kind who gave, without question, out of love.

Chapter 20

Phoebe tugged her sleeves on her blouse down around her wrists and brushed down the front, straightening out a wrinkle and brushing off a piece of string.

She hadn't worn this blouse in forever, but it was a deep green color that complemented her eyes, and it also flattered her figure, at least she thought it did, when she wore her pencil skirt with it.

Maybe she was a little dressed up to go to the chamber music concert in Sweet Water this evening, but a few days ago, she had mentioned it to Tillman and just casually asked if he'd like to go along.

She hadn't thought of it as a date and hadn't really considered telling him about it before.

He said that he had heard about it and wouldn't mind going at all, and in fact, he'd pick her up and take her.

It…felt a little bit like a date.

Her hands trembled as she took one last look at herself in the mirror. She looked fine, like a woman in her mid-thirties going to something a little bit fancy.

There were streaks of gray in her hair. She could see them even without the light on overhead.

When had she started to get gray? She typically didn't pay too much attention to her hair at all. She definitely hadn't while she was homeschooling her siblings. Life had just flown by, and she hadn't even noticed. Sometimes they didn't even celebrate her birthday because she didn't even remember. There were just…other things that were more important.

But now, now that she was maybe hoping to catch the eye of the best man she'd ever met, she saw all the imperfections, the crow's-feet at her eyes, the blotchy, old skin of her face that makeup didn't really even out. She could have layered it on a little more, but she had never been good friends with makeup, and it typically didn't look the way she thought it did when she went out with it on.

She probably shouldn't have tried at all, but she did put some eyeliner and mascara on. It made her eyes stand out a little more and gave a bit of color to her face so she didn't feel quite so washed up.

Forty wasn't that far away. And forty was…old. Really, really old.

Of course, thirty-six was old as well. She could definitely be termed an old maid.

Except, she felt young and almost like she might giggle at any moment. Surely that put her in the category of a schoolgirl?

Except were they even called schoolgirls anymore? She was definitely old.

Everyone else had left, and she was the last person down the stairs. Her siblings and she would all support Claudia with her chamber music, and some of her siblings had actually picked up their instruments and gone to practice, playing in it just to support their sister if nothing else. Although they all enjoyed playing.

It was something their mom had insisted on. She had a background in music, and every child of hers had an instrument thrust into their hands almost before they could walk and had been expected to be diligent about learning to play throughout their childhood.

Some of them had been more diligent than others, but Claudia had been the most diligent of all.

She played several instruments and also had the background in music. Which didn't exactly come in handy on the ranch, except now that they had a dude ranch, and they sat around the campfire singing songs with their guests, it actually was useful.

Who would have thought?

Wouldn't her mom be smiling now if she could look down through the windows of heaven and see her children going to a chamber music concert, with most of them playing in it?

The thought had Phoebe smiling as she stepped out on the porch. Tillman had pulled up and parked his pickup, getting out and walking up the steps.

"That's a pretty smile," he said.

His compliment made her smile grow bigger.

"I was just thinking about how happy my mom would be to see all of her kids going to a music ensemble led by one of her daughters. With some of them playing in it too. I think she'd be pretty happy."

"So it's because of your mom that Claudia has her gift of music?" Tillman asked, holding up the bouquet of wildflowers that she hadn't noticed in his hand.

"Oh my goodness. They're beautiful!" she said, taking them from him as she turned toward the door. "You can come in while I put these in water," she called over her shoulder.

He followed her in, saying, "They're just wildflowers. I saw them earlier today and thought of you, and I had a little bit of extra time so I grabbed them after I was ready."

"Well, it's special. I'm embarrassed to say how long it's been since anyone's given me flowers," she said, finding that she felt a little teared up. Pushing those thoughts out of her head, she focused on the question that he asked. "You said about Claudia having her gift of music from my mom, and it's true she does. But Mom taught all of us to play instruments, so you could say all of the Clyborne music is because of Mom."

"That's a good gift to give to your children. A gift that keeps on giving."

"Yeah. One that we can use all our lives. When I was younger, I wanted to do gymnastics so bad. I watched the Olympics on TV and was enraptured, but we just couldn't afford lessons. It was too expensive. And I'm not really built as a gymnast anyway. You kinda have to be short. I might have been okay as a figure skater, but I'm too tall for gymnastics."

"I don't know about that. You're very graceful anyway."

"I know you're just trying to make me feel better. But it's okay. After I got older, I realized that it wouldn't have worked out, and I would have wasted a lot of time. I would have spent time on something that I couldn't use past my teens or maybe my twenties if I was very diligent. But music… I can use that for the rest of my life. So can my siblings. And I'll always think of my mom and be grateful that she insisted. I didn't always want to practice."

"I've heard that's the hardest part."

"Some people love it. Claudia always was very diligent in practicing, and she seemed to enjoy it. Something about the repetition? I'm not sure, but I didn't have that love, and I hated sitting still, but I wanted to listen to my parents, so I pretty much forced myself. Which, again, I'm glad I did."

"I'm sure you are. Kind of makes me wish I could make my kids practice an instrument, but…" His voice trailed off, and she felt bad for him but knew there was nothing he could do.

"Have you heard anything?" she asked softly as she arranged the flowers in a vase on the table.

"Not really. I've been talking to them every evening, and about three days out of five Nicole has not been up to get them off to school. I don't think she's figured out yet that they're calling me. I told them not to tell her. I hated to do it because I don't think children should keep secrets from their mom, especially at that age, but I was afraid that she would be angry. And I didn't want the children to be the object of her wrath when I'm the one who deserves it."

"You don't deserve it," Phoebe said, turning with her brows drawn.

"Yeah. You're right. Just I'm the one who's doing the thing that she'd be mad about, but instead of being mad at me, she'd be mad at them."

"You haven't heard anything about the boyfriend?"

"No."

He didn't seem to be overly upset about it. It was on the tip of her tongue to ask how he felt about Nicole and her boyfriend and the whole situation and if he had the opportunity, would he go back to her?

She supposed it didn't matter. The evidence that he felt something for Phoebe, something more than…more than he felt for other people anyway, was right in front of her as she arranged the cheerful flowers.

"Thank you so much for these. They're beautiful."

"I didn't realize it was going to make you smile so much. I…feel like I'm getting a little more credit than I deserve for them, but you're welcome. It was my pleasure."

Yeah. He did it as a nice gesture. She should not read anything into it.

She tried to remind herself of that as they walked toward the door, and she went out again.

He walked with her to the truck, opening her door, and she murmured a thank you.

"You know, no matter how many nice things I do for you, you never stop saying thank you. I guess it doesn't matter, but it makes me feel like you appreciate it every time."

"I do. I hope I don't get to the point where I don't appreciate the kind things that people do for me. That… That's just paying attention to the little things, right? It's the little moments that make a life, not the big ones. Although we have a tendency to think it's the other way around."

"That's a good point. It's the little moments that make life." He spoke like he was thinking. "So that's why you pay attention to the little things?"

"I guess. Or maybe partly because of my parents too. I spent some time in regret, wishing that I had been kinder or more appreciative of the things that they did. It's an eye-opener whenever you don't have them anymore and all the things that you didn't realize that they did are now in your lap. Not that I did it by myself, Ezra was there, and of course Priscilla too."

"I see. So it's just the events of your life that taught you to appreciate the little things."

He closed her door and walked around. When he got in, she asked, "Why are you asking about that? About where I learned to appreciate the little things?"

"Just some people don't, you know?" He shrugged, backing up and turning around and starting out of the driveway. "Some people don't seem to notice what anyone does for them. They never pay attention, and other people seem to notice every little thing. You are a detail person, but even people who notice physical details sometimes don't notice what other people do."

"Maybe it's something we train ourselves for."

"That's what I was trying to figure out. I like it. I wish I was more like that, and if I get an opportunity, I'd like to teach my children to pay attention to people. To be grateful. To appreciate the little things."

"I think sometimes parents really aren't deliberate about the things that they want to teach their children." She gave him a rueful glance. "Speaking as a sister who ended up raising my younger siblings. We go day by day, and we get sucked into the catastrophe of the moment, the chaos and fighting and the bickering and nothing ever seems to be what anyone wants and we're tired and we forget that we actually had things that we wanted to pass on to our kids. And it's not usually in the big moments that we pass them on. We think we'll sit everyone down and we'll be like 'okay, guys, this is your lesson for today.' But that's not when they learn. It's in the times the kids look at us. How they observe us. They watch us, what we do, and it's day in, day out, those little moments that teach our children whatever it is that our lives show. And usually that's not what we want to teach them. It's just what comes out."

"That's pretty deep." She almost thought it could have been a sarcastic comment, but he said it in a way that made her think that he was actually thinking about it and that he really did think that it was something worth pondering.

"I obviously don't have children, but I did raise my younger siblings. And all the mistakes I saw my mom making, I thought, 'oh, I'll never do that,' but I ended up doing the same things. And while

I was at it, I tried to figure out the things that Mom and Dad would want to teach them. And I realized that they'd already picked up a lot of those things. Not because anyone had ever taught them, but because they'd seen us older kids modeling those behaviors."

"This makes me really uncomfortable. Because I know that my children's most vivid memories of me are probably me yelling at their mom. I'd like to justify that and say any sane man would have gone ballistic with things that she had done, but I don't want my kids thinking that's okay behavior. And you're right, I can sit there until I'm blue in the face with them sitting down in front of me and me teaching them the right way to behave, but when they see me responding in the right way, that says so much more than hearing me tell them how it should be."

"Yes, exactly, and seeing us respond in the wrong way teaches the exact opposite thing of what we want to teach them, but we don't realize it."

"It seems so obvious, we should surely know it, but again, life happens in the little things in the small moments, and we have a tendency to miss it."

"Hmm. I was just thinking today about how life flies away. I can't believe I'm as old as I am, and I don't know how I got here. I feel like I should be about fourteen. But I'm more than twice that old."

"Life does go by fast," he said thoughtfully as they pulled into the church where the chamber music concert was going to start in just a few minutes. "It seems like it's really packed," he murmured as he drove to the back end of the parking lot to find an open space.

"I'm so happy. When Claudia first started, she could hardly get anyone to participate, and it was a real struggle. She was kind of discouraged and a little depressed, and maybe that's how she and Beau finally got together. He started helping her with this."

"It must be really good."

"I think she just chooses fun music, and yeah, they practice a lot and there's some really great stuff."

"You wouldn't expect that from a small town."

"No, and I think that's what Claudia was thinking when she did it. Sweet Water could use this. After all, it's a great place."

"I saw that this past week when your barn burned down. That wasn't a good thing, and don't think that I think it was, but it really impressed upon me the way this community comes together and supports each other. It wasn't just people giving money, although that would have been really nice, I'm sure, but it was people giving of themselves, their time, their talent, the things that they own and sharing them. Helping out however they could. Whether it was food or a dump truck, it was all here."

"It was pretty amazing, wasn't it?"

"It made me think about what kind of man I am."

"That's probably a good thing. When we stop and think about how we want to be better, how we want to change, how we want to approach the world and our spot in it. Do we want to just observe? Talk about the things that are happening? Or do we want to put our boots on and go help?"

"Exactly. And obviously, I was helping, but I was being paid for it. There were a lot of people who were there who weren't being paid, and I wondered if that would ever be me."

"It doesn't have to be a community-wide thing. It can be just something that you do for someone else. A little bit of grace. Giving mercy, a smile even."

"Food is easy. Am I allowed to say that women have it easier than men?"

She laughed. "I don't think so. After all, there are a lot of people who need help moving or with odd jobs around the house, like cleaning their gutters out, and maybe they can't afford to hire someone, that are definitely things men can do better than women, although I certainly know how to clean out gutters."

"I didn't doubt it for a minute."

They grinned at each other, and then they got out, meeting at the front of the truck and walking toward the church.

"I've really enjoyed the time I've gotten to spend with you." He lifted his shoulder and looked around ruefully. "I just wanted you to know. You're a great person, and I admire you a lot."

His comment warmed her to her bones. She tried to be casual. "Thanks. I've admired you as well."

She did not tell him that she specifically admired his shoulders, and his walk, and the way the muscles of his forearms rippled when he worked.

Of course she admired other things in him, like his character and his integrity and his desire to be better, but she grinned a little because those weren't the first things that came to her mind.

Of course, maybe they weren't the first things that came to his mind either, her character and her integrity and all those other things. She might not find it so funny if he admitted that to her.

Chapter 21

Phoebe and Tillman went into the church, having a little bit of difficulty finding a seat, and finally found one toward the middle of the church in the middle of a row. People shuffled and moved in order for them to sit down.

"Well, I guess everyone saw us walking together. Sorry about that," he said. "I wasn't exactly intending that."

"It doesn't bother me. But if it bothers you, I can get up and sit somewhere else?" She didn't really intend to be smart about it, but she didn't know why he was apologizing for sitting with her. He was the one who turned her invitation around and said that he would take her. Maybe he was getting cold feet.

"I just don't want people to talk about us if that's not what you want."

"I guess I wouldn't have said I would go with you if I didn't want that. Not that I'm looking for that, but no, it doesn't bother me."

She met his eyes, her gaze steady. She was thirty-six years old. She wasn't going to pretend she wasn't saying what she was saying. She knew he had a lot of baggage, a lot of things to work out, and she respected that. But at the same time, she liked him. And she wasn't going to pretend she didn't.

"All right then," he said, a corner of his mouth picking up. "You've seen me pretty much at my worst. I wasn't expecting you to think better than that about me."

"I've seen you work. I've seen you try to be better. I've seen you with your kids. And I've seen you making decisions that are difficult. Of course I see you as better than your worst."

How could he even think otherwise?

They turned, facing the front as the musicians gathered and began to tune their instruments.

The performance was magnificent, and Phoebe was sure everyone left with a smile on their face. Including the musicians. But most especially her sister Claudia. She was so happy for her, that her dream of having a chamber orchestra had worked out. Claudia had put so much time and effort into it, and had worked so hard, and this was a wonderful fruit from all of her labors.

It was slow going as they went out, grabbing a few refreshments before they left and chatting as well.

Phoebe had to admit to having a wonderful time, and as nice as the music was, a lot of her enjoyment was because Tillman was with her.

They left together as other people began to drift away as well.

The area around the church was lit, but they walked beyond the circles of light to his pickup toward the back of the lot.

The first time their hands brushed, Phoebe thought it was an accident, but then his fingers brushed hers again and slowly wound around them.

"Is that okay?" he asked, looking down at her and lifting their entwined fingers.

"Yes," she said, hearing how breathy her voice sounded.

He swallowed. "I've…been thinking about this for a while."

"Me too."

They didn't say anything more as they reached his truck and he opened the door for her. Their fingers slipped apart, and he seemed like he was reluctant to let hers go.

She was not the one getting out of a bad relationship. She was not the one with nasty memories, with two children who hadn't been in a stable home, and who wasn't allowed to see them unless she drove six hours to them. She was not the one with the anger and bitterness, and so she supposed it was all about what he thought he was ready for.

She didn't want to pressure him, but she had to admit, she liked this evening. The sweet, thoughtful flowers, the fun time they had together, leaving with their fingers entwined.

Plus there was the laughter and the fun she shared with him throughout the week. Maybe Ezra really had tried to get them together. She had never asked, but it might be a good question. After all, she hadn't seen it to begin with, but she would have to agree if anyone said that Tillman seemed like he was perfect for her.

They didn't say much on the way home, although his hand slid over across the seat and touched her fingers as they lay in her lap.

She twisted her hand and turned it over until their fingers threaded together again. This time was just as thrilling as the first. As if she would have ever thought that holding hands with someone could be thrilling. But it was.

The big house was all lit up when they got home, but Tillman drove past that, and while he didn't pull up to the bunkhouse exactly, he parked a little bit between the two.

"Do you mind taking a walk with me before you go in for the night?"

"I would love it," she said, meaning every word.

He grinned, shut his pickup off, and got out. She slid out too, wondering if he really wanted to walk, or if he had something he wanted to talk about.

That time when his hand slid into hers, she was expecting it and maybe even had moved her hand in position to make sure that he did.

She might be older, but she still had a few feminine wiles that she could pull out when the occasion demanded it.

"You know my life is a mess." Tillman's voice was low, and it floated softly in the air as Phoebe looked up at the stars that shone so brightly in the cloudless sky. It was chilly, and she wouldn't have minded having a jacket, but she didn't want to interrupt their conversation to go back and get one. There was a part of her that wanted to have everything settled, and there was another part of her that admitted that it probably wasn't going to happen. It wasn't quite going to be the way she wanted it to be with everything tied up with a neat little bow and everything figured out perfectly.

"I know."

"And your life is perfect."

"I wouldn't say that, but I definitely have less drama in mine than you do unless you count money drama. I have plenty of that."

He laughed a little. "I have some money drama myself. Along with all the other drama. None of it fun."

"Drama usually isn't fun. But every life has some."

"That's true. But it seems like my life has had more than my share."

"And you handled it well and have become a better person. Maybe I would be a better person if I had more drama in my life."

"You lost your parents, that was drama."

"Ezra hinted that your early life wasn't the greatest," she said, keeping her voice pitched naturally but hoping that maybe he would expound on that.

"I don't think there's too much to say. My dad was abusive. Lots of kids grow up with that type of thing. Alcohol, marijuana occasionally. He hit my mother and me. Although he typically left my little sister alone. Mom left him when I was about ten, the first time he hit my sister."

"I didn't know you have a sister."

"She died of a drug overdose about ten years ago. Broke Mom's heart. Mom died shortly after. I guess my old man is still around, but he was never really a dad to me. I haven't looked for him."

"You still managed to become a man of character despite the terrible childhood."

"Maybe because of it. Definitely because of my mom. She cared about what happened to me and tried to instill all the good teaching she could, although I had a hard time believing that Jesus loved me when my dad didn't."

"I could imagine that would be tough. I never doubted my parents' love. They might have been taken from me too soon, but love wasn't something I lacked."

"I can't say the same. But I did have some friends whose parents had some good marriages, and I always wanted one that looked like theirs, you know?"

"Yeah. That makes sense."

"I thought Nicole was the one. Obviously, I was wrong, and you know all about that so I won't go into it, but probably some of my upbringing came out in my marriage. Yelling, for example."

"It's hard for me to imagine that."

"I've tried really hard to modulate my tone and my emotions. That's what it is. Something gets you so angry you can't control yourself. The time to stop it is before you get that mad. I… I tried to change the way I talk to myself. If I start feeling angry, I ask myself, is this worth getting angry about? Is there another way to solve this? Just stuff like that. I can't promise that I'm going to be perfect."

"No one can promise that. I told you, I yelled at my siblings. I had to do pretty much the same thing. Figure out the kind of person that I wanted to be and then work on being that person. And not allowing myself to be the person that I was becoming."

"Yeah. Thanks for understanding."

They kept walking, the buildings falling way behind them, some chatter from some of the ranch guests carrying across the night air in tones they couldn't understand.

Being that it was the middle of the week, they didn't have too many guests, and the ranch almost felt deserted.

"I guess I wouldn't be walking in the moonlight holding your hand and asking you to talk to me if…if I didn't have some pretty strong feelings for you."

She didn't say anything to that, because that was exactly what she had thought. That there must be something going on to inspire him to want to talk to her.

"I don't typically go around walking and holding hands in the moonlight either."

"I didn't think you did. I guess that's why I think it is probably important for me to declare my intentions."

She was curious as to what those intentions were, so she waited, trying not to hold her breath.

He stopped, turning and tugging on her hand until they faced each other.

"Phoebe."

She shivered at the sound of her name on his lips. It sounded more perfect there than anytime anyone else had ever said it. She wanted to ask him to say it again, but she lifted her head instead and searched his eyes, waiting.

He pursed his lips and looked over her shoulder for a moment before he looked back at her. "I did something like this once before, with one other woman. You know that. I feel a little bit like…like I screwed that up,"

She wanted to tell him that it wasn't his fault, but she kept her mouth closed. She didn't really like being reminded that she was the second one who had stood in the moonlight with him. She could tell him that he was her first. But this didn't really feel like the time. He seemed like he regretted things, and while she had regrets in her life, that wasn't one of them.

"I don't want to cheapen what's between us." He paused. "It feels like a cliché to say that I feel different with you than I ever have with anyone else, but while it might be a cliché, it's also true. What I felt with Nicole was just a shadow of what I feel with you. I… I admired the wrong things about her. The way she looked, the way she filled out her clothes, the way she was a little sassy and didn't care. For some reason, I found those to be things to admire. I feel like I was never really taught what was important in a relationship, and I didn't see it for myself until I met you."

That made her feel a little better. That he could see a difference between her and Nicole and see things in her that he admired more. That she wasn't just his rebound relationship, or a substitute, or the first woman who happened to come along who responded to his overtures of affection. After all, she wasn't exactly experienced in this area, and someone could easily take advantage of her. She wouldn't even know it.

But she didn't think that Tillman was that kind of man. She wouldn't be standing here with him otherwise.

"I'm not doing this very well, but what I'm trying to say is…I love you. I love watching you. I love being with you. I love seeing you first thing in the morning, your smile, the coffee you're always holding close, and the way you're wide awake, even though I'm still half-asleep and not quite ready to talk for at least three hours. And you don't get impatient. I love that about you. That you see me, and instead of seeing me the way I see me, you see me as someone…better. You make me want to be better." He stopped, then continued like he had started and wasn't going to quit until he was done. "I want to be with you. I want to spend my life with someone who makes me better, makes me want to be better, and who…maybe I inspire in some small way as well."

"You do. You absolutely do."

She didn't expound upon that. It seemed to be his turn to talk, but he smiled at her words. And his hand came up and brushed her hair back away from her face.

"I can't even believe I'm here with you. You know I have nothing. I mean, I have absolutely nothing."

"I guess you know I'm not here with you for your money then," she said with a small smile. Then she continued, "And I'm pretty sure you're not after mine, since you know as well as I do that I don't have any either."

"I think we can build something together, though. Am I wrong?"

"I've never worked with anyone who I enjoy working with more. And yeah, I think we can build something. Between us, I don't think either one of us will give up."

"We can build a family, business, something. As long as we're together, I don't really care what it is."

"That sounds perfect to me. I'll be beside you, helping, building, and wanting to be better, because that's how you make me feel."

He grinned a little, and his hand slipped down and wrapped around her neck. She tried to suppress a shiver. A good shiver, as her hands came up and settled on either side of his stomach. She leaned closer.

"I don't want to rush anything, but I want you to understand that this isn't a fling for me. I… I've never been good at relationships that weren't serious. I'm not ready for marriage, just yet. I have so many things that are tangled up I can't even begin to untangle everything, but that's what I'm looking at. At some point, hopefully not too distant in the future. I don't think relationships should drag on. It's too tempting to do things you shouldn't."

"That's what my parents always said."

"It's what my mother told me, although she also cautioned me not to rush into anything."

"Sounds like your mother was a wise woman."

"She was. I wish you could have met her. She would have loved you. She would have been over-the-moon happy for me. Although, maybe she would be shaking her head, as I would like to, wondering how in the world I got to the place where someone like you is looking at someone like me and thinking that I'm a good choice for you."

"An easy choice," she said softly.

She smiled up at him, and he looked down, lowering his head. "I'll do everything in my power to make sure that you don't regret this."

"There won't be any regrets. Not on my end," she said, feeling confident and knowing that what she said was right. Whether Ezra did it on purpose or not, she knew he wouldn't have brought Tillman here if he hadn't felt like Tillman was a good fit for their farm. Not only that, but what Tillman had said about her making him better fit with the idea that she had been thinking that she was a better person when she was around him. Not only did she admire him, but she felt like they could definitely build something together and was sure, down to the depths of her soul, that the Lord had brought them together.

As his lips descended on hers, she sighed a little, a contented sigh, mixed with a little bit of excitement and a lot of nervousness.

She moved a hand up, wrapping it around his head and pressing herself closer to him, while he pulled her closer as well. Like they both had the same thought at the same time, which was not uncommon in their relationship.

The dark was perfect, the night filled with stars that seemed to shine down just for them.

When he finally lifted his head, both of their breathing was ragged and they seemed to cling to each other for strength just as much as because they couldn't get close enough.

"You are perfect," he said, his breath blowing out, his words sounding like they had been taken from his soul.

She moved her head, rubbing her cheek against his rougher one and running her thumb down his neck. "I was thinking the exact same thing about you. In every way."

She didn't get a chance to say anything more, because his phone rang. It was late enough that a warning bell went off in her head. Then when he pulled it out of his pocket, keeping one arm around her, and she saw the look on his face, a whole bunch of warning bells rang.

Of course, life couldn't be perfect for too long. But whatever it was, she was sure of one thing, they would face it together.

Chapter 22

Tillman fumbled for his phone. For the first time in his life, he felt like he was in the perfect place at the perfect time with the perfect woman in his arms. He should have known that he didn't get the perfect life.

But he pushed the thought aside, because maybe, God just wanted to try him a little. And make him better. He knew there was a lot of room for improvement.

So he tried not to resent the interruption and instead focused on the encouraging idea that if Phoebe said she had chosen him, she wasn't going to change her mind. Because that was the kind of woman she was. The kind who stuck to her word and did what she said she was going to do.

He saw the number and frowned. It was the number that his kids had been calling from, but…it was late. They should both be in bed.

"Hello?"

"Daddy, I don't feel good."

It was Erin, and she sounded terrible.

"Where don't you feel good at?" he asked, immediately concerned, his heart already beating fast because of the kiss he'd just shared with Phoebe but now pounding rapidly for a different reason. Fear.

"My stomach. It hurts."

"Where at?"

"On the side."

"Which side? The side on the hand that you write with?" He was trying to think of which side hurt when someone's appendix was about to rupture.

"Yeah."

"Did you tell your mom?"

"She told me to shut up and go back to bed."

"Did you get Rowan to go down and tell her that you don't feel good?"

"Rowan tried after I went down, and she yelled at him too. She's… She's drinking that red stuff, and it always makes her mean."

He wasn't sure exactly what the red stuff was. Probably wine.

"The house smells funny, and Daddy…" She started to cry. "I hurt so bad."

"All right, baby. You just hold tight. I'll try to call your mother, and if she won't answer, I'm going to have the ambulance coming to get you. So you stay right by this phone, you and Rowan both, so if anything happens to you, Rowan can answer."

He didn't know if she would pass out from the pain, but if her appendix was about to rupture, she needed help and she needed it fast.

"Okay. Daddy?"

"Yes, baby?"

"I'm scared."

"All right. I can understand why you would be. I can't talk to you too much right now, because I have to make a call, but I'll pray, and I know that Jesus is with you."

He wished he had been able to spend more time with his kids, telling them that Jesus really was with them, not springing it on them sometime when they were afraid and didn't have any clue who He was.

"Call back, Daddy."

"I will, baby."

"Bye."

All the time, Phoebe had been staring at him, concern on her face. She didn't have to tell him that she was praying silently beside him. He could feel it. There was just something in the air, something that made him feel brave, and competent, and somehow know that everything was going to be okay, even if it didn't feel like it was. And even if things didn't turn out the way he wanted them to.

He pulled Phoebe tighter with one arm as he used his other to dial Nicole's number. He still knew it. It was etched in his memory. It had been the number that he had called all through their relationship, anticipating with excitement the idea of talking to his girlfriend and then his wife.

No longer. Dialing the number now gave him a nasty feeling in the pit of his stomach. It turned putrid when she didn't answer and the call went to voicemail. He tried once more, with the same result.

"I'm calling 911."

"Good idea," Phoebe said, and then she was quiet while he talked to the operator who answered. She had to patch it through to the operator in the area where his family lived, which took a little bit of time, and he tried not to be impatient. They were doing the best they could, and him getting upset wasn't going to help anything. Maybe later, he would be proud of himself for not losing his temper or flying off the handle at anyone or anything, since he stayed calm throughout.

It was the Lord, and maybe Phoebe's prayers.

As soon as he knew for sure that they were sending someone, and the operator told him most likely it would be a life-flight helicopter which had been dispatched, and it would be taking his daughter to a hospital that could do the operation immediately, that's when he hung up and called his kids back. He didn't want the lights and the sirens and whatever else might be happening to scare them.

"Hello?"

"Erin, baby. Are you okay?"

"It hurts, Daddy."

"I'm sorry." He flinched. Was there anything harder than knowing someone he loved was in pain and he couldn't fix it? "I've got people coming to help, but it's not going to be me."

"But I want you!" And she started to cry again.

"Rowan?"

"Daddy?"

"You're going to have to be brave and help your sister. There are going to be some lights, sirens maybe, and you won't know the people who are coming into the house. You're going to have to let them in. Can you do that?"

"I guess so. Are they bad men, Daddy?"

"I wouldn't let bad men come in. But you're going to have to unlock the door and let the good men in so they can take your sister to the hospital so that she can get better."

"But I don't want her to go! I don't want to be by myself!"

"I'm on the way, little man, but it's going to take me a while. I'm not going to be able to get there before she leaves, so you're going to have to be brave. Just for a little bit."

"But I don't want to be brave! I want to be with you!"

"I will have you with me as soon as I can." He tried to figure out what to do. "Hang on a second, just hold on, I'm going to get my truck, but we can stay on the line. Okay?"

"Okay."

He looked at Phoebe, her face resolute, knowledge already in her eyes that he was going to have to leave, and she was going to have to stay. He wanted to take her with him, but he didn't think that was a good idea. He had no idea what he was going to get into, and she would need to stay and help on the ranch, keep things going with the rodeo.

"I want to ask you to come with me."

"I want to go." But she didn't make any move to. "But I think it's better if I stay. I… I don't want to hold you back or hold you up."

"You wouldn't."

"If you want me to go?"

"I do, but I think you're right. We still have the rodeo to do, and we've already been sidetracked with the fire, now this. I'll do everything I can from the hospital room."

Assuming his daughter lived. He prayed hard she would.

"That's fine, we've got the notebooks, I know exactly what's going on with you, because we spent so much time talking about it. I'll pick up and do what I can, but please don't worry about me. You stay with your kids. That's where you need to be, for as long as you need to be there. And secondly, I love you too."

She reached out and pressed her lips to his, and he almost forgot that he was in a hurry to leave, because he wanted to wrap his arms around her and pull her tight, deepen the kiss and make it last longer. But she pulled back almost as soon as it started and said, "Be careful."

There was so much more he wanted to say, so much he wanted to do, so much time he wanted to spend in her arms, but none of that could happen right now. He nodded, put the phone back to his ear, and strode away.

Chapter 23

Four days later, Phoebe held her phone tightly in her hand and walked out to the same area where she and Tillman had shared their first kiss.

She'd talked to him several times on the phone, and she thought that things were actually working out for him, although her prayer was that he would do the right thing. That he would show loving compassion to Nicole. As much as Phoebe wouldn't mind having Nicole completely out of the picture, since she represented Tillman's past, someone he had been intimate with, someone he had done the same things that he had done in the moonlight with Phoebe. She didn't really want that reminder in her face all the time, but God loved Nicole too, and in Phoebe's mind, Nicole was struggling.

"Hey there, sis." Phoebe turned to see Tobias walking up to her.

Of all of her siblings, Tobias was the one she could really use as a sounding board and a fount of wisdom. He had been working almost nonstop on the structures that needed to be built for the rodeo. Several fences, a good many pens, and he had made the concrete forms that would help support the job johnnies.

He also had been making hay in the area where they were going to have folks park.

She hadn't spoken with Tillman much about the rodeo; everything had been about Erin and how she had been doing, the custody of the children, and Nicole.

"Hey, Tobias. It's good to see you. You've been working really hard."

"I've enjoyed it. Although, I have some things I need to do with Mrs. Wells that I've been putting off because of this. So once the rodeo is over, you might not be seeing me much."

"I heard her granddaughter was coming to live with her." She'd forgotten about that in all the hubbub of everything else happening.

Tobias was silent for a bit, and then he said, low and slow and so casually that Phoebe almost missed the implications, "She is. I might marry her."

Phoebe had to do a double take.

"Do you know her?" To her knowledge, she'd never met Mrs. Wells's granddaughter before.

"No."

"I thought you said you might marry her."

"She's in a tough situation, and marrying her will solve some problems."

"That's a crazy reason to get married. You can't have a marriage based on…solving some problems."

She clamped her mouth closed. Tobias didn't need her lecturing him. He needed her support, her encouragement, her standing shoulder to shoulder with him, knowing that he had someone beside him who would support him no matter what. He didn't need her censure or her discouragement.

"I know. Sometimes I think Mom and Dad would roll over in their graves if they knew what I was doing. But I can't shake the feeling that it's the right thing to do."

"If it's the right thing to do, Mom and Dad would be behind you one hundred percent."

"I suppose only time will tell."

She hated to say anything more, so she tried to keep her mouth closed. But Tobias deserved a good woman. After what he had been through, he deserved someone who was going to love him the way he would love her and be completely devoted to her.

Tobias, of all her brothers, would make some woman an absolutely amazing husband. He was as close to perfect as a man could be. And that was from someone who had lived with him as close as people could be for years. Tobias was the real deal, he was loyal to a fault, considerate, kind, and somehow always able to figure out what the people around him needed and then find a way to give it to them. The world needed more men like Tobias. She hated to see him throw himself away on… "Did you say she had children?"

"Yeah. Four or five. I'm not sure. There are a couple different dads involved. It's a mess."

Phoebe clamped her tongue between her teeth deliberately. Hard, until she tasted blood. She was not going to give him a hard time. Was not.

"If there's anything I can do to help you, let me know. Once the rodeo is over, hopefully life will settle down a little bit."

"Actually, I think your life might get more interesting."

"It might," she said, and she couldn't keep a little smile off her face. Now that they knew that Erin was out of the woods and was going to recover—she'd been taken out of the ICU yesterday and was likely to be released from the hospital tomorrow—everything else would work itself out.

At least she hoped it would.

"You want to talk about it?" Tobias asked easily, hooking an arm over the fence as he leaned a hip against it and looked out in the pasture at the black forms of the cows milling about, munching on grass, one of the most relaxing sounds in the world if Phoebe had anything to say about it.

"I don't know that there's really anything to say. I'm happy for Tillman, because Erin is going to be okay. And he has Rowan with him. Apparently there was some kerfuffle with the child services when they found that Nicole was passed out, either drunk or high, no one was really sure, and they released Rowan into Tillman's custody. Then there was an emergency meeting between the judge and the two lawyers. Nicole lost custody at that time, and now Tillman has charge of both children."

"That's exactly what he wanted, isn't it?" Tobias asked easily.

"Yeah. But Nicole's a mess because her boyfriend broke up with her, which apparently is what led her to do what she had done that caused her to not notice that Erin was not just sick but deathly sick."

She took a breath. She knew she needed to be fair about it. As much as she wanted to be hard on Nicole for her choices. Especially what her choices were whenever her children were in her custody. Phoebe had never walked in her shoes, and she could hardly be the one to judge. Other than she knew that children should be protected at all times.

"I know Tillman is struggling because he sees an opportunity to be exactly where Nicole was with him. Where he gets full custody, and she can visit the children if she drives the entire way to see him and then only have supervised visits."

"You don't think that's fair?"

"I don't know. I just want Tillman to make a decision based on, first of all, the safety of his children, but from a place of kindness and compassion, and not out of anger and bitterness. He… He has the opportunity to pay her back for every unkind thing she did to him with the children, and I think he wants to be better than that. I want him to want to be better than that."

"I see. That kinda surprises me. I would think you'd want the ex out of the picture."

"Oh, I do. So I'm struggling in my own heart. Because…it would be really nice if he was able to get full custody, and Nicole had nothing, and we could try to be a family together without her. It's…what I would prefer but not what I think is necessarily right."

"I think that it's pretty mature of you to be able to see that."

"I know that some people get divorced, and their exes get along with their current spouses, and everything is just hunky-dory and A-OK, and I guess I'm just not like that. I don't want to have a weird marriage where I'm married to my husband and his ex-wife is a big part of our lives, and…I suppose that's the adult thing to do, but sometimes I don't feel very much like an adult."

"I think we all sometimes come to a point in our lives where we want to just be children, selfish, immature, and do what makes us feel good, rather than doing what makes the most sense, or what is best for others, or, in this case, the children."

"Yeah. I guess I just wish that if the Lord was going to give me a beautiful love affair, He would give me one that's clean with no mess, you know? Give me a man who doesn't have kids, who doesn't have an ex, doesn't have a whole lot of baggage…except I love Tillman. And I want him. And he comes with an ex and with baggage and with drama and with everything else that seems to be a part of his life, and I need to love all of that too and accept it and do my best with it."

"Well, I think you've come to the right conclusion anyway. Or at least you know what the right thing to do is. Now, it's just a matter of getting yourself to do that."

"How did you know?"

"Sometimes I struggle with that too."

"I wouldn't have guessed it. Everything always seems so easy to you."

"Maybe I'm good at acting differently than how reality is. Because, things are hardly ever easy for me."

Her phone rang, and she pulled it up immediately, hoping it was Tillman and relieved when she saw it was.

"I'm heading back. Let me know if I can help you any," Tobias said, touching her shoulder before he walked away, his hands in his pockets, his head pointed down to the ground, shoulders slumped.

She wondered what he meant about marrying Mrs. Wells's granddaughter, and the idea of his wife having children to several different fathers, and him getting himself into a mess… Tobias was always so levelheaded. He said he hadn't even met her, so it wasn't like he could have fallen in love with her. What was he thinking?

And…was he going to leave the ranch?

She shoved that thought aside, intending to bring it back out sometime when she could think about it, as she swiped on her phone, putting it to her ear and saying, "Hello?"

"Hey, sweetheart."

She smiled. She thought that she loved her name on his lips, but sweetheart was even better. "Hey there. I've been hoping you would call."

"Yeah, sorry. I just got done talking to the doctors. They're going to discharge Erin first thing in the morning. Rowan and I are sleeping at the Ronald McDonald house, and I was planning on coming back to the ranch as soon as we're out of here."

"Of course."

"Erin might need a little bit of extra attention. I…"

"Don't worry about it. If she needs nursing care, I'll do it, you can do it, or anyone on the ranch will help us."

"I know you gave me a full update on how things are coming for the rodeo this morning, any news?"

"Nothing new. Tobias worked all day making hay, and the field is completely cut and cleared. We're ready to put up the one-wire fencing to keep the cars in. We should have enough acreage for twenty thousand cars. If there's more than that… They might have to park along the road."

"Let's hope they do. That's what I want, more than what we anticipate or expect."

"I love how you're so gung ho about it."

"I've had a lot of time in the hospital to spend on the phone, and I've been calling everyone I know. I've got a lot of confirmations, and the buzz is all over social media. That doesn't cost us a thing."

"No. But the things that did cost us, the flyers, a couple of billboards, and a few spots on the radio, have all been paid for, and we're getting a lot of interest on the website that Sondra made."

"That's awesome. I think it's going to be bigger than we even anticipated."

"I hope so. We could really use some good news."

"Well, talking about that, I talked to my lawyer just before five this evening, before the doctors came in, and I didn't have a chance to call you with the news."

"Okay?"

"I want to talk to Nicole, and I want you to be there with me. They… They feel pretty confident that I can get full custody, and Nicole will be relegated to supervised visits. It'll probably be a year or more until she could hope for anything else. That's if I want to throw the book at her. Or…we can figure something else out."

"Do you think she's safe? As in, do you think she's going to go downhill again?"

"I'm not sure. She called me before the lawyer did, and she was sobbing, begging me to take her back, apologizing for blowing up her family, and…"

Phoebe felt fear screech through her. Tillman had the opportunity to put his family back together. She should encourage him to take that opportunity. The children would love to have their mom and dad together. To be brought up in a home where both parents were there, loving them and taking care of them.

"I don't want to lose you. But…maybe that would be for the best."

"No. It is not. I made that mistake once. And I do believe that she's sorry for what she did. But I don't believe she's changed. She hasn't apologized for any of that. And I haven't seen any kind of change in her. Plus, our divorce is final. She was with someone else. There is…no going back. Not for me."

"Are you sure?" she asked, part of her sad for the children. But if Nicole hadn't changed at all, it would not be best for them to be put through that again. Where their mom and dad got back together, and then they broke up again as soon as Nicole found someone she liked more.

Not that Phoebe was sure that that would happen, but it sounded kind of like Nicole hadn't had a fundamental change, just she was sorry that things didn't work out in her favor.

"My main concern is she can't be smoking weed and watching kids. Especially not while she's drinking an entire bottle of wine. I knew she had a bit of an affinity toward alcohol, which I suppose is fine if that's her thing. People drink alcohol all the time. But the problem is, alcohol is one of those things that can get away from you pretty fast and screw things up even faster. It… It's probably better to stay away from it, because once things are screwed up, they're really hard to put back together."

"You would know," Phoebe said, knowing that Tillman had already been through it once.

"Anyway, Nicole and I had a long conversation, and I just basically said that I wanted to do the right thing by her. I didn't want to keep a mother away from her children. I… I didn't want to invite her to live out at the ranch, because I thought that would not be good for us, but I did tell her that perhaps her moving to North Dakota could be a fresh start for her, and we would be closer, so it would be easier to share custody of the children, once she was cleared by professionals saying she no longer had a substance abuse issue."

"That was wise on your part. The safety of the children should be first."

"That's what I told her. I… I've been thinking a lot about what you said a few weeks ago about being filled with anger and bitterness and needing to let that go in order for God to fill me with something else. Without that, without prayer, then God helping the bitterness to leave, I might not have been ready this afternoon, but I was able to tell her that I didn't want her to be shut out of her children's lives. I wanted her to be as involved as she wanted to be, but that had to be after she took care of herself."

Phoebe felt tears pricking her eyes. Tillman had handled that way better than she would have suspected he ever could. If she had given him a script, she couldn't have given him a better one.

"I'm so pleased with you. So happy that you were able to rise above your circumstances and instead of treating her the way she treated you, treating her better. Showing love and compassion. You're an amazing man."

"It's because of you. I told you, you make me better. I wouldn't have been able to do it if you hadn't pointed me to Jesus. That's what I needed. Someone to show me that the way I was living wasn't the right way. Even though I knew it, I just needed that push. That nudge toward the Lord, and that was all you."

She appreciated the fact that he was giving her credit, but he didn't understand that it took the right kind of man, the right kind of attitude to take a push like that and do what was right with it. He had.

"I love you."

She could hear the smile in his voice when he answered, "I love you too. I can't wait to see you again. I can guarantee you I'll be looking you up first thing when I get there tomorrow."

"Maybe I'll be waiting for you."

"All right. I can take that."

Phoebe smiled in the darkness. She'd never felt like this before. Maybe it was the infatuation phase of falling in love, and perhaps the feelings would fade eventually, but it didn't matter. Whatever they eventually settled into, she knew that Tillman would stand beside her for the rest of her life. And that was all she really needed. That and Jesus.

Chapter 24

It was a beautiful day. There had been a small scare a few days earlier when the weather had forecasted rain for the day, but the forecast had changed, and the high was supposed to be close to eighty, with clear skies all day long. The next day was supposed to be even a little warmer, with the same clear skies. Two days, perfect weather. God couldn't have been better to them in any way.

Phoebe stood on the steps, holding Erin's hand as they watched the first cars pull in. Tillman was already out, directing traffic, doing some last-minute preparation, and helping livestock trailers to back into the right pen.

The Baldwin family had allowed them to use the auction lot in town to house some of the animals, particularly the ones they were going to be using tomorrow.

Everything seemed to be falling into place.

Phoebe had been up hours before the sun, cooking and getting things ready. They had a lot of vendors who were selling food, crafts, and other miscellaneous items, but she was selling food to make money for the ranch as well. Over the last week or so that Erin had been on the ranch with them, Phoebe had done a lot of sitting by her bedside, and then as Erin got slowly better, they had walked hand in hand around the ranch, stopping and watching Tillman work for a good while, which was something Phoebe would never get tired of and Erin seemed to enjoy as well.

Phoebe felt like she bonded with Erin better than she ever would have been able to if Erin had come to them not sick.

Tillman had enrolled Rowan in school already, and Rowan had seemed to fit right in, taking to it like a duck to water.

Phoebe was thankful for the little things, the way things had been coming together, in all areas. The judge had even called an emergency session that had given Tillman full custody. It was up to him to decide how much Nicole got to see the kids and how often.

The last Phoebe had heard, Nicole was planning on moving out to North Dakota. She had a job at the diner if she wanted it, and there had been a room for rent above the hardware store.

That wasn't super thrilling to Phoebe, and she could feel Tillman wasn't exactly ecstatic about it either, but they both knew what was best for the children, and they would welcome and encourage Nicole as much as they could. But Tillman had made it clear that part of his life was behind him and Phoebe was his future.

The only thing that bothered her was that there seemed to be something bothering Tillman. The last two days if she looked at him when he wasn't aware of it, there seemed to be a worry line between his eyes, and his face was a little tight.

She only noticed because she spent so much time studying him that that slight change made a big difference to her.

She had asked, casually, if there was something wrong, and he'd answered her quickly, too quickly in her opinion, that everything was just fine.

She wasn't sure exactly what it was, but it had cast a cloud over what should have been one of the best days of her life.

"You said I could help you with the food, right?"

"You sure can, honey," Phoebe said as she looked down at Erin. She had taken a chair out to the booth where they would be, and she hoped that she would be able to get Erin to spend some time in it. She didn't want her to overdo it. Even though her recovery had seemed to be going without a hitch.

Rowan was stuck to Tillman's side, and she smiled as she watched the father and son walk across the parking area, talking to a cowboy, while Tillman gestured toward the paddock and the parking area they had designated for trucks with trailers.

Whatever was bothering him, she supposed he would tell her eventually. But she was worried it had to do with Nicole, and maybe he was regretting his decision to walk away from that and create a new life with Phoebe. Maybe he had figured that the opportunity to have a regular family, which his children most assuredly would want, was right in front of him, and maybe he thought he was making the wrong decision.

Lord, please give me the strength to want all the best things for these kids. Help me to be able to give up what I want, in order for them to have a happy life. If that's Your will.

She meant that with all her heart.

Smiling down at the sweet little girl beside her, she said, "Are you ready?"

"Yep!" Erin said with a big nod of her head.

Phoebe smiled again, and they set out across the yard, ready for their big day.

Chapter 25

"What do you mean you don't think I should drive?" Jim asked as Agathe gripped the keys tightly in her hand. He held his palm out for them, but she couldn't bring herself to drop the keys into them.

"I just… I just thought it was a good idea for me to do it," she said, trying to sound cheerful and hoping that he didn't go off on one of his anger-induced, verbally abusive rants. The kind of rants he never had back before he started to succumb to Alzheimer's.

"Now, Agathe," Jim said in a cajoling tone. "You know I always drive. And you ride with me in the car. That's just something a man does for the lady he loves."

She smiled. It was her old Jim, speaking in a tone of sweet cajoling that made her feel loved and appreciated. Something she hadn't been feeling much of lately.

But she still didn't want to give him the keys.

"How about you let me do something for you for once?" she asked, smiling and showing him her dimple, and feeling a lot younger than she had for a long time.

"I do. I let you cook for me every day. And I appreciate it. That's something you do for me. And while you weren't a very good cook when we first got married, I've got you trained just about right, now."

She grinned. It was true. She hadn't been a very good cook, even though she'd come from France, and every American she'd ever met expected her to be able to make French cuisine like it was something she was born knowing how to do.

"You're so sweet," she said, running out of ideas of how to distract him. He still had his hand out, although he had put his other arm around her and pulled her close to him. She snuggled down deep, holding on to his waist with one hand and her keys with the other. Feeling right at home where she had been for decades, snuggled up beside her Jim.

"Now give me those keys, girly. I'll take you wherever you need to go. And you know, all you have to do is say so."

"I know," she said, trying not to let the tears that were pricking her eyes fill them and definitely not allowing her voice to crack. She didn't want any telltale signs that her heart broke every time he said something like that. The Jim she knew and loved wasn't who she saw much anymore, and the man that he'd become, who didn't know her and she didn't recognize, had taken his place.

Maybe it was because of that that she held the keys out and dropped them in his hand. She didn't want to fight with this Jim, the one she hardly ever got to see anymore. Not that they'd ever fought. So seldom she really couldn't remember any specific time. Maybe just a few arguments here and there. But he'd always treated her with so much love and respect, like she had done him the greatest honor in the world when she agreed to marry him and moved across the ocean to live in his country.

It had been a big change, and maybe it had been a big sacrifice if she looked back on it, but she had wanted to do it because she had loved Jim with all her heart and soul, and she believed he had felt the same about her.

She had been right.

She hadn't known this was going to happen. This fading away where one hour he knew her and then the next two hours he didn't.

"That's my girl," he said, dropping a kiss on her forehead as he squeezed her even tighter, and she relished the feeling, knowing that the day would come when he wouldn't recognize her at all, ever again. And she would never be tucked up against his side, him dropping loving kisses on her head, his arm around her, and calling her girly.

"Now, where are you taking that casserole again?" he asked as he opened the door and she got in.

"To our neighbors, the Clybornes. They lost their barn in a fire, and I wanted to do something nice for them. They spent so much time helping me—" She broke off abruptly. They helped her by watching her husband so that she could go to the Alzheimer's support group meetings.

She didn't want to even talk about it. In his more lucid moments, she and Jim had talked about the fact that he had Alzheimer's and that he was fading away, once or twice. But she didn't want to ruin the few good times they had left by talking about something that depressed him every time. He hated the fact that he didn't know who she was and didn't remember not knowing or anything about those things that happened when he became the man she didn't know.

"I need medicine, so I can drop you off at the post office first, and then I'll pick you up after I grab my medicine, and we'll go on out to the farm together. Will that work for you?"

"Yes." She spoke against her better judgment, even though the post office was right beside the drugstore in town. There really wasn't much that he could do that would mess anything up. Surely the ten minutes it would take for him to drive to the drugstore and pick up his prescription, which should be ready, and then go back across the parking lot and pick her up at the post office would not be enough time for anything terrible to happen.

"I'll be right back," he said as they stopped at the post office, and she got out, carefully making sure that the casserole was still sitting on the floor behind her seat.

"All right. I'll be waiting for you right here," she said as she turned to go into the post office.

He would be fine. She could see the drugstore from here. He knew he was going to the drugstore, he knew she was at the post office. There wasn't anything more for her to do.

"Goodness gracious, if it isn't Agathe. It's been a long time since I've seen you in here. Usually I have someone in here picking up mail for you, or buying stamps for you, or dropping your mail off, but here you are in the flesh."

"Yeah. It's me. My husband dropped me off," Agathe said, maybe bragging a little, because how many more times would she be able to say that? Would this be the last?

"Did you hear what happened out at the Clybornes'?" the postmistress said, leaning over and lowering her voice like she was imparting state secrets, rather than saying something that the entire town had to have known, since Agathe herself knew it. She, in her caretaking state, was the last to know anything nowadays. So if she knew, they could be sure that everybody else in town knew as well.

"Are you talking about the fire?"

"Yes! It was started by some teenager standing behind the barn smoking a cigarette and just tossing it over his shoulder like he didn't have a care in the world. What are the youth coming to nowadays?" the postmistress said, in a tone that said that the world was going to hell in a handbasket.

Agathe already knew that. She'd been experiencing it for the last eighteen months as her husband slowly faded away from her.

She spent longer than she expected talking to the postmistress, and it had been a good ten minutes until she walked out. Even two years ago, her husband wouldn't have been upset if she took that long. He was used to people talking and chatting, and he never got impatient with her. It was like once he retired, his entire world revolved around doing whatever he could to serve her and make her life happy. Like she had done for him all of his working life.

Except, lately, it was impossible for him to be what he wanted to be, and that made her sad too. It was so hard to see her strong, capable, handsome husband, who always had a joke and a kind word, falling to fits of rage, not knowing where he was, flirting with women he would never have flirted with before, and walking outside without his clothes on, among other weird things he'd done.

She hurried to the door, opened it, and her heart leapt up into her throat. Her husband was not there.

Surely he was at the drugstore. Maybe there had been a delay. Maybe he forgot his wallet. She hadn't thought to ask, and he shouldn't have needed it, other than to maybe present his insurance card. She took care of all the business she could over the phone or online, and really all he had to do was drive through the pickup window.

But there was no car in the parking lot that matched the description of their car.

What in the world was she going to do?

Chapter 26

Waylen pulled into the post office, squinting. Was that Agathe?

He smiled, but his heart felt heavy. She was going through the exact same thing that he had gone through not that long ago. The pain and the long, hard days, and the heaviness that settled over him, the darkness too, were way too fresh.

He probably would never forget watching his beloved wife slowly leave him. Some days, she knew him, some days she didn't, and he wasn't sure which days were harder.

All the time, he wanted to cry, and he had never been a crier.

He had been totally and completely in love with his wife and hadn't ever looked at another woman, not ever. Now that she was gone, even now, more than a year later, it was hard to get into the idea that he was free to look if he wanted to. He had trained himself for so long to not.

And then Agathe had walked into the support group meeting, just as he was about to quit going. He didn't need it anymore, and while he felt like his wisdom and experience was helpful, it could also be discouraging, because he had spent so long…he didn't want to say waiting for his wife to die, but that's kind of how it was.

Since she wasn't herself anymore, they didn't have a husband-wife relationship. Once she got to the point where she no longer knew who he was ever, the days were long, hard to fill, and it was hard for him not to…wish that things would hurry along. He couldn't admit that to just anyone, because people who had never been there wouldn't understand.

Not that he wanted to lose her, because he didn't, but he already had. The shell that was her body didn't contain the woman he loved. He couldn't tell anyone what the medical terminology was, he just knew that for the last several years he took care of his wife, it wasn't really his wife.

But it was her body, and he had pledged his life to her; whether she was inside that shell, or whether she wasn't, the only thing he could do was to keep his vows.

Now, his eyes had been taken by Agathe, but…she had all these years of agony ahead of her. And he wasn't getting any younger. But he also knew, from the years that he'd spent alive on the earth, that he was blessed to have had such a beautiful marriage the first time around. Most people were not blessed with one marriage like he had, let alone two. And yet he felt like he could have a second one with Agathe.

The problem was, she wasn't ready and wasn't going to be for a long time, so he had determined to be a friend to her.

That was harder than it seemed. The line between friends and more got blurry at times, and while he wanted to be her shoulder to cry on, her rock, the person who helped her when she needed it, he couldn't keep his emotions from getting involved. At his age, he would have thought that he wouldn't have had trouble with that type of thing, but he definitely wanted to be more than friends.

Shoving all those thoughts aside, he parked in a spot near her, and she didn't even seem to notice. She was just staring at her phone, looking like she was having a panic attack in place.

He opened his door and got out and took the two strides to her, closing the distance between them and putting a hand on her shoulder.

"Agathe? Are you okay?"

She didn't flinch at the touch of his hand, but at his voice, her head jerked up.

"Waylen!" she said, like she had been on a deserted island for thirty years and he had just come to rescue her. "Oh my goodness. I am so glad to see you. I've lost my husband. He has the car!" She ended that last sentence on a wail, and he knew exactly how panicked she was.

"Hold up. Start from the beginning. Where was he going?"

"Right there." She pointed to the drugstore across the parking lot. "He dropped me off at the post office, he was supposed to go through the drive-through window and come right back. He wasn't going to be gone but three minutes, five tops. I ended up talking for ten. I didn't mean to, but there was the fire at the Clybornes—"

"I know. Sometimes you just get caught up in conversation." Especially when a person was stuck at home, caring for someone who didn't recognize them. "So it was ten minutes that he's been gone?"

"I must've been standing here for five. So fifteen minutes."

"All right. I'll call the police."

"I don't want him to be in trouble. He hasn't done anything wrong." She lowered her voice. "At least not yet."

It had that tone in it that said that she was well aware that in the state that he was in, he could cause all kinds of problems.

"I didn't mean to give him the keys. I mean, I didn't want to. But he was…he was himself!"

He patted her shoulder. Totally understanding. As his wife slowly left him, the few times that she was herself, he didn't want to do anything that might cause an argument and turn her into the person that he didn't know. He could well imagine Agathe being the same. Jim being all kind, like he always had been, and her not wanting to rock the boat.

It might be time for him to go to a home, but Agathe was probably just like him and wouldn't want to give the care of the person she pledged her life to to someone else. Not while there was still breath in her body and the ability for her to do it.

Not that it was wrong for anyone else to make that choice, it just wasn't a choice that he could make. He had said he would take care of his wife in sickness and health, and he would do everything in his power to keep that vow.

He could imagine Agathe felt the same.

He had dialed 911, and the operator picked up. He briefly explained what was going on, and she said she would dispatch a trooper who was in the area as well as alert local authorities. They would be watching out for the car, and someone would find him, she assured him.

He thanked her and then hung up. "They are looking for him now. If you want, you and I can look for him, too."

"Oh. Do you mind? I don't want to keep you from anything if you're busy."

"I'm retired. My whole day stretches out in front of me, and I can do whatever I want to." He was busier now that he was retired than he had been before, although in the months after his wife died, he had become somewhat of a recluse. He supposed that was normal. He was…not shocked that she died, it was just hard to face the fact that she was never getting better, never coming back. That he was alone. Permanently.

Except, he wasn't, or he didn't need to be. He could find another woman. Not just anyone, someone with whom he had the opportunity to have a second chance at love. It seemed a little selfish since his first chance had gone so well, but when Agathe walked in, he knew that she was the one.

But sometimes when a man saw a woman he knew he wanted, it wasn't the right time.

He didn't want to covet another man's wife, and he wasn't sure where the line was there between right and wrong. He had wondered that at times himself when he was taking care of his own wife, who was his wife, of course, but her mind wasn't there. She wasn't being a wife to him, and he had been lonely, sad, and longed for the companionship that a wife provided.

He hadn't talked about that to anyone, not even at the support group. And definitely not to Agathe. He supposed the vows, "as long as you both shall live," said it all. Even though he wanted to split hairs and make it right to find companionship somewhere else.

He would never encourage her to break her vows or do something that she was uncomfortable with. She wouldn't be the woman he admired if she was willing to do so.

But since he first started talking to her, no other women came close to being what she was, and he had decided that it might be better for him, even though he had a limited amount of time left, to wait for the right one or not have one at all.

Of course, he assumed that she felt the same way about him that he felt about her, which he did not want to talk to her about, because that could open a can of worms that they might never get closed.

Since he'd managed to make it through his entire life without once committing adultery or fornication, he didn't want to start when he was the age that he was now.

He was closer to meeting his Maker than he ever was before, and he wanted sin to be behind him.

So for now, he would help her find her husband—he had confidence her husband would be found—and he would support her however he needed to, even if that meant just being friends.

Chapter 27

The first day of the rodeo was a huge success. A bigger success than Tillman had dared to dream it could be. There had been far more than the twenty thousand cars they had room for, and he and Tobias had spent some of the day working on getting a place for more people to park.

Phoebe had been scrambling for food, and she had several huge deliveries slated for first thing in the morning, so they were ready to start again tomorrow, since they had run out of almost everything that day.

God had been better to him than he deserved, he knew it. But as he slowly closed the door on his sleeping children, his eyes fell on the letter that sat on his dresser.

It was a bill from the hospital.

A bill he had absolutely no ability to pay.

It was worth it, because without the services of the hospital and the life flight, the doctors had said if Erin had been even an hour later they might not have been able to save her. Then there was the ICU stay and the regular hospital charges.

It all added up to far more than he could ever hope to pay. If he hadn't already lost the ranch, he would be forced into selling it to pay. But as it was, there was no way he could come up with the money to pay that bill.

He didn't know what to do. He could hardly ask Phoebe to share her life with his when he would be starting out with a bankruptcy, which was the only thing he could see that he could do in order to solve the problem. And that grated on every nerve he had. He had never had a bill that he hadn't paid in full.

But he didn't have health insurance with his job, and Nicole had let the state health insurance that she had gotten for the children lapse. She hadn't talked to him about it, and he had had no idea.

He had been fighting just to see them, she certainly wasn't talking to him about anything remotely concerning their health or the school or anything.

He hadn't known. But he had been the one to call the ambulance, and the bills were written out in his name.

He didn't know what he was going to do. But he supposed God knew. And while he was trying not to worry about it, he also knew that he needed to just let God work. And God would work with the bill. Even if it meant Tillman would be forced to declare bankruptcy.

The thing that he didn't want was to drag Phoebe into that mess. She didn't need to marry him and have her credit completely ruined because of a bill that had nothing to do with her.

He knew she didn't have the money to pay either, since the ranch was just trying to stay solvent, hence the rodeo.

Lord, I don't know what I'm going to do about this. But You do. I know You have something in mind. And if that means I have to give up Phoebe, in order to protect her from this, please make it clear to me. Because, if there's one thing I don't want, it's to lose my children or Phoebe. In fact, Lord, I want her to marry me. But it feels selfish to ask her to marry me when I have this hanging over my head. You know, God. Please make it clear to me. Amen.

He had already said good night to Phoebe. She was practically dead on her feet, and she had promised to keep an eye on the kids if they didn't wake up with the sun in the morning. They had strict instructions to find him or Phoebe as soon as they woke. Everyone else on the ranch would be keeping an eye out for them, too. And while there was the potential for there to be bad actors anywhere, most of the people who were at the rodeo seemed to be good people who were looking for some family entertainment.

Tomorrow was another day, and he would try to put this worry to bed, and think about the things that he could do something about, and leave the things that he couldn't do anything about in the hands of the Lord.

Chapter 28

"It feels a little weird not having our morning and evening meetings," Tillman said as he walked along the lane in the dark, holding Phoebe's hand.

Phoebe could have said the same thing.

"I've missed our meetings." They'd still seen each other every day. At meals, for sure, and in the evening after Tillman put his kids to bed, they usually took a walk as they were doing now. Sometimes Phoebe took the kids into the house and helped them with their schoolwork or made supper with them if Tillman was working and couldn't get away.

"I think I like this better," he said as he squeezed her hand.

There still seemed to be something bothering him, but Phoebe hadn't figured out how, exactly, to ask. She didn't have anything concrete to point to, just a general sense of knowing that he didn't look as relaxed and happy as he had before everything went down with Nicole and the kids.

"I heard Nicole starts work at the diner tomorrow."

"Hmm."

He didn't say anything more. She knew talking with her about Nicole wasn't his favorite pastime, but when he didn't talk to her about Nicole, it made her feel like maybe there was something he was hiding, something she was missing. And that, combined with the feeling that there was something wrong, made her chest feel heavy and scratchy.

"There's something I need to talk to you about."

Thank you, Jesus, Phoebe thought silently. Maybe they could get whatever was bothering him out in the open. Even if it wasn't what she wanted to hear, she'd rather know, so she could figure out how to deal with it and work together with Tillman to do whatever needed to be done.

"I wondered when you were going to bring it up."

"You know?"

"No. I just knew there was something wrong. Something that's been bothering you since before the rodeo."

The rodeo had been a bigger success than either of them dreamed, mostly because of Tillman working tirelessly, not only to get things ready on the ranch, but to get the people he knew would draw a crowd to come. Even in the hospital, he'd been working the phone, getting buddies on board, and doing everything he could to get things to work out.

She had been so impressed with how he'd pulled everything together. Ezra had confided to her that he'd never imagined it could work out so well.

The barn debris had been cleared away, leaving a cleared dirt area where the charred wood had been, and the Sweet Water community had indicated that they would come help with a barn raising, although they probably would just put up a pole building. It was cheaper and quicker.

"You should have said something."

"I was…afraid."

"Afraid? Please don't ever be afraid to talk to me."

"You don't like talking about Nicole, and I can tell you get irritated when I bring her up, and I was scared that after she begged you to take her back, you felt like being with me was a mistake, or at the very least, it would be better for the kids to be with their mom and dad and for you two to be together."

"That's nonsense! I have zero desire to be with her…we talked about that."

"I know. Maybe sometimes I need to be reminded. People change their minds, you know. All the time."

"You're right about that. Even though I'm tempted to say that will never, ever, not in a million years happen to me, I see that you might need reassurance. Even on a regular basis. Even though I don't see a need for it, because I know how I feel about her—and that's blessed to be away from her." He paused for a moment and then continued. "Do you remember how you told me that sometimes we need to get rid of the bad things in order to make room for the good?"

"Yes."

"And I think we also talked about how Nicole blowing up my life and family was the worst thing that ever happened to me, mostly because I lost my kids and the ranch I'd worked for my whole life."

"I'm so sorry about that."

He tugged on her hand and pulled her around to face him. "Don't be. I was thinking about that just last night. I wouldn't have met you if it hadn't been for losing the ranch. God really did have something better in mind for me. You. And I kicked and scratched and fought to keep it, not knowing that keeping it would keep me from the best thing that ever happened to me—having you tell me you love me."

He swallowed and looked into her eyes. Maybe they were a little watery, mostly because she was so happy for him, but also because he had said such wonderful and amazing things to her and she could hardly believe that the man she loved thought so much of her.

"Well, you can talk to me anytime if those are the kinds of things you're going to say."

"Actually, I do have something that's not good news." He hesitated. "Something that could change things for you."

She couldn't think of anything that would change things for her, other than Priscilla going to Wyoming, but Priscilla had just told her the day before the rodeo that she had decided to stay. For now. That allowed Phoebe to assume she was going to stay, although she still prayed daily for her twin.

"Okay?"

"I got the bill for Erin. With the life flight, and the ICU stay, along with the regular hospital charges…it's more than I can ever dream of paying."

"I can't even imagine."

"I was surprised. For sure. I thought I might have to declare bankruptcy, and I still might. But I talked to the hospital, and they said I could set up a payment plan. It's just… I still had a dream of having a few acres and a house and a place for us and Erin and Rowan…and any other children we might have…"

His voice trailed off. She could feel her cheeks heating, although maybe it wasn't the best time to admit that she really, really wanted more children. A big family like she'd grown up in. But he was going to worry about how they could afford it.

"But with that huge bill to pay, I probably won't be able to afford much of anything. I don't even know if I could plan on moving out of the bunkhouse." He squeezed her hands, and she came toward him, feeling like he'd prefer to move away, but she wasn't going to allow that. No matter what happened, whether they had plenty of money or not enough, more children or just two, a place of their own or sharing the bunkhouse, the place she wanted to be was right beside him.

"Phoebe…I can't ask you to be with me if I don't even know how I'm going to take care of you."

"Can't? Or don't want to?"

"I can't."

"Then you want to?"

"Yes! I want you with me, forever. I hate being away from you, and I want to marry you and have a family with you, but I just can't—"

"Then do it. You didn't see how God was going to work out losing the ranch. Or how He was going to bring things around after Nicole left. We can't see how He'll work this out or even if He will, but I can see how He worked things out for us to be together. I'm not going to miss that opportunity just because I can't see how God is going to work it out now."

He blew out a long, slow breath, a little smile tilting up his lips. "I need you. God knew it. And I know it, too."

She smiled as his head lowered and he kissed her tenderly, sweetly, pulling her close and holding her tight.

He lifted his head, touching her temple with his lips and running his hand down her back. "I want to marry you."

"It's a little late tonight. How about first thing in the morning?" Her words were breathless, but she didn't even care. Tillman was the one she wanted, the one she knew was God's plan for her life, and she'd take him however she could get him.

He laughed. "Did you not hear me that I have, literally, nothing?"

"I don't care." She laughed. "Unless you care that I have, literally, nothing?"

He chuckled, tucking her head under his chin and holding her close. "We're a pair."

"We are."

"So I guess we should make it official."

"I agree."

"Tomorrow might be a little soon."

"The next day?"

"Let's see what tomorrow brings. Maybe it is perfect. As you are for me."

Chapter 29

"I saw the bill sitting on his dresser when I went to check the kids for Phoebe." Tobias paced back and forth in the small room Ezra used as an office. He'd been thinking about the hospital bill he'd seen in Tillman's room for several days since the rodeo had ended and they'd tallied their net profit.

It was more than enough to get the ranch in the black and keep it there for the rest of the year.

"You're sure the insurance isn't covering it? Sometimes they send out statements with the breakdown included."

"I thought I might have seen wrong, so I just casually asked Tillman while we were taking the parking fence down if he'd switched his insurance from Montana to North Dakota, and he said Nicole had let the insurance on the kids run out after she left him."

"Ouch. So it's not even his fault."

"No. He could barely get her to let him see the kids, let alone have any say in anything, including their insurance." Tobias stopped in front of the bookshelf, staring at the spines of the books there but not actually seeing them. "I know we've struggled for a long time with the ranch, and this seems like the lift we need to finally take the burden away, but…I feel that we should pay that bill for Tillman, even if it means we don't have anything left for ourselves."

"We'd have to ask the rest of the siblings. I couldn't just do that without their permission."

"I know. I know what Phoebe will say. And I have a feeling that Phoebe has done so much for everyone else, all the time, selflessly, that no one would keep this from her. Especially since they're getting married this morning."

"Does she know about this?"

"I think so. I didn't ask her outright, but she said something about being with Tillman was more important than money. I think she knows and she wanted him anyway."

"That sounds like Phoebe. I would be concerned about a normal couple since money issues are one of the top things that lead to divorce, but Phoebe has never insisted on anything for herself, and she's always given sacrificially. This is our opportunity to give something to her—Tillman is the one thing she wants."

"I hope he knows what a treasure he has."

"I think he does. It's hard to work with Phoebe the way he has and not see it. I knew that when I put them together. Of course, I didn't realize this was going to happen with his daughter. I agree with you. They deserve the money from the rodeo more than anyone I know. We'll call a meeting while they're in town and see what everyone else says."

Tobias nodded and pulled out his phone on his way to the door. He wanted to get everyone together and make a decision before Tillman and Phoebe got back. If the decision didn't go in their favor, it would be better for them not to know they'd considered it at all.

He needn't have worried. The siblings took less than five minutes to unanimously decide that Tillman and Phoebe should have Erin's hospital bills paid. Someone also suggested if there was anything left over, they should give it to them so they could find a small place close to the ranch or build a house on the ranch property, since the bunkhouse wasn't exactly a newlywed paradise.

Tobias felt a little like his chest would burst, even though he had the dread of what he knew he needed to do hanging over him, still. Mrs. Wells was expecting him to save her granddaughter, and he'd promised the old woman he would. Unfortunately, there was only one clear way to do that, and it entailed him leaving his family and marrying a stranger.

He wouldn't have even considered it if he hadn't gotten that strange letter in the mail. He'd looked into it, the best he could, talking to some of Sweet Water's wiser citizens, and he'd been assured by Sawyer Olson and Ford Hansen that the letter was, indeed, real.

Which meant Tobias could keep his word to Mrs. Wells and next week this time, he could be married to someone he'd never met.

Chapter 30

"I can't believe what your siblings did for us." Tillman curled a piece of Phoebe's hair around his finger, loving the silky feel of it over his skin and on his chest.

She snuggled closer, her arm around his waist, her legs tangled up with his. "I can. They're the best, and I can count on them for anything."

He thought that they could count on her for anything as well and probably had over the course of the last decade and a half since their parents had been killed. But what a way to reward Phoebe's faithfulness in giving up any life she might have made on her own as she took care of her younger siblings, homeschooling them, raising them, and devoting her life to making sure they had a stable home and family.

"You deserve that…and so much more." He turned his head and kissed her temple, wondering what it would be like to be married to her for decades and always knowing that God had given him far more in his wife than he ever deserved.

"I don't deserve anything but hell," she said. "And yet, God gave me you. I am the most blessed woman in the world."

She could think that if she wanted to. He knew it wasn't true. But it made him feel like a million bucks to think that's what she thought.

God had taken something he thought he wanted more than anything away from him, and He'd filled his life up to overflowing. He couldn't imagine having more. But then the Clybornes had paid off Erin's hospital bill, and they'd given them even more so they could build or buy a house.

Phoebe wanted to build. A house and a family. She had wanted to get started on the family right away. Who was he to tell her no?

He grinned. He would have fun making a family, and he'd grow and become better with Phoebe beside him as they raised them together.

"Tillman?" she whispered, her breath flowing over his skin and making him shiver in the very best way.

"Hmm?" he said, his fingers running down her arm and over the soft skin of her waist.

"I love you."

"I love you, too, sweetheart." His lips found hers, and he kissed her for real, wanting to show her just how much.

A Gift from Jessie

View this code through your smart phone camera to be taken to a page where you can download a FREE ebook when you sign up to get updates from Jessie Gussman! Find out why people say, "Jessie's is the only newsletter I open and read" and "You make my day brighter. Love, love, love reading your newsletters. I don't know where you find time to write books. You are so busy living life. A true blessing." and "I know from now on that I can't be drinking my morning coffee while reading your newsletter – I laughed so hard I sprayed it out all over the table!"

Claim your free book from Jessie!

Escape to more faith-filled romance series by Jessie Gussman!

The Complete Sweet Water, North Dakota Reading Order:

Series One: Sweet Water Ranch Western Cowboy Romance (11 book series)

Series Two: Coming Home to North Dakota (12 book series)

Series Three: Flyboys of Sweet Briar Ranch in North Dakota (13 book series)

Series Four: Sweet View Ranch Western Cowboy Romance (10 book series)

Spinoffs and More! Additional Series You'll Love:

Jessie's First Series: Sweet Haven Farm (4 book series)

Small-Town Romance: The Baxter Boys (5 book series)

Bad-Boy Sweet Romance: Richmond Rebels Sweet Romance (3 book series)

Sweet Water Spinoff: Cowboy Crossing (9 book series)

Holiday Romance: Cowboy Mountain Christmas (6 book series)

Small Town Romantic Comedy: Good Grief, Idaho (5 book series)

True Stories from Jessie's Farm: Stories from Jessie Gussman's Newsletter (3 book series)

Reader-Favorite! Sweet Beach Romance: Blueberry Beach (8 book series)

Cowboy Mountain Christmas Spinoff: A Heartland Cowboy Christmas (9 book series)

Blueberry Beach Spinoff: Strawberry Sands (10 book series)